Up The Ladder...and Over The Top

ISBN 1-59109-641-3

Up The Ladder...and Over The Top

Memoirs Of A Hollywood Studio Musician

Bob Alberti

2003

Up The Ladder...and Over The Top

TABLE OF CONTENTS

ACKNOWLEDGEMENTS

This book began with random thoughts from past experiences, as I recalled the many humorous situations I'd encountered through my years in the music industry. It grew beyond my wildest imagination in scope, and as a first-time scribe I realized I had reached a dead-end. *Where do I go from here?*

Without the help of my wife, Shirley, it would still be at that point. Her critical eye for printed errata and a sense of flow allowed me to compile my thoughts in reasonable fashion. She was invaluable in her assistance.

I also owe a debt of gratitude to former high school classmate Lee Alperin. His expertise as an English instructor and author gave guidance in development of the fragments contained in the original manuscript.

Sandra Coutsakis, a personal friend and former neighbor, was instrumental in guiding me through the preparatory steps on the road to publishing the final product.

My heartfelt thanks to all.

Front cover design by Nancy Beiman

PREFACE

In the bygone era of live television shows, live recording sessions and large orchestras, there was a class of musicians who were considered elite. They became known as *studio musicians* or *session players*. They were generally the most versatile members of the American Federation of Musicians, able to walk into nearly any situation and play what was there on sight. All styles were required, be it swing, bebop, classical, jazz, country or rock. One didn't have to be the all-time ace but had to know enough to stylize appropriately for the arrangement or the artist. From my earliest awareness of session players, it was one of my career goals. With persistence it eventually came to me, partly through luck and partly through my ability to handle the tasks as the opportunities arose. The one caveat is, like an athlete, a studio musician has a limited time-span of popularity, since musical styles and concepts change quite rapidly, as do the upcoming generations of musical trendsetters.

The long-standing irony of the studio musician's career goes something like:

1)"Who's Bob Alberti?"

2)"Get me Bob Alberti."

3)"Get me someone who plays like Bob Alberti."

4)"Get me a young Bob Alberti."

5)"Who's Bob Alberti?"

To explain the irony: 1) When a musician is new to the Los Angeles music scene, his ability is spread around by word of mouth via musicians with whom he may have played an inconsequential job. The contractors who do the hiring for the leaders of studio orchestras are usually dubious of unknown and untested newcomers. They tend to question the new name in town.

2) Eventually you'll land a session, probably as a last-minute substitute for an established player who failed to show up. Once you've done a couple of sessions and are seemingly lauded for your ability, then all the contractors want your services. You become the new "whiz-kid" in town.

3) A few years into the Hollywood scene when you're working three sessions a day, seven days a week, the contractors begin to assume that you're always busy, and they start looking for some new sound-alikes, i.e., people who play in a style reminiscent of yours, and who have similar abilities.

4) After a few more years the youth movement begins to take shape, and the newer, younger group of television and record producers are hesitant to have too many gray-haired or balding musicians in the orchestra.

5) After about ten or fifteen years on the scene the musical styles have changed, as have the mode of dress and the hairstyles. Another musical generation has arrived. The new crop of session players are on the scene, and you realize you have made it to the top of the ladder, only to end up going over the top into oblivion.

With the rapidly approaching designation of "senior," which is the seventy mark, I thought that while I still have a relatively accurate mind and my memory bank is still functional, I'd put down on paper the events, people and places that shaped my career. I've often been told by associates that I should write about some of the inside anecdotes that occurred throughout my years in the music business. Whether these insights will be of any interest whatsoever to anyone other than my immediate family or an occasional close friend remains to be seen. It nonetheless is a catharsis for me, and it manages to take up some spare hours of time as I hunt and peck along my computer keyboard.

I could never be accused of being well read, nor do I have a particular skill for following a literary format in writing. I liken my style to the manner in which I speak, or to use a comparison, it's more like the capsulated *USA Today* than the detailed *New York Times*. I'm usually concise, to the point, and then get on with it. I can sometimes be abrasive with my directness, not intentionally but more so as I've gotten older. If I have an opinion about something, I intend to deliver it, and if there are consequences, I'll willingly accept them. Occasionally I've been referred to as a *curmudgeon*, and I won't deny that there's an element of truth in the reference.

Throughout the various chapters, I make mention of my mother, not always in glowing terms. I survived a turbulent relationship with her over the years, a relationship which steered me into years of therapy. Happily, I survived and surmounted her alcoholism and the obstacles she presented, coming through it as a stronger human being.

I'm very happy to have my own personal counterbalance, my wife Shirley. Without her love, encouragement and willingness to pore over this plethora of words, it probably would even be less understandable than it is. She has a sense of literature that far outweighs anything that I may have garnered over the years. Her time was spent in Hollywood as a television script supervisor, so inaccuracies and errata in any written form send off well-trained alarm-bells.

The music world is as political as any business or government. There were years of turmoil as I grew into the music business, but through those years came a zillion laughs. The overall balance fell in my favor as I managed to accomplish everything that I had set out to do, and even more. I consider myself extremely lucky to have made a living doing something that I love to do, which is playing and writing music. My goals were playing jazz, being with some of the best big-name bands of the 20th century, arranging for records, television and film, plus being personal accompanist and conductor for many artists whom I grew up admiring. The following chapters will take you through a chronological sequence of the life of a pianist who is proud to have accomplished everything he desired, foibles, flaws and triumphs not withstanding!

CHAPTER 1

PIES LIKE MOTHER USED TO BAKE
AND TARTS
LIKE FATHER USED TO MAKE.

A ringing telephone at four o'clock in the morning can set one's adrenalin racing. Mine was no exception as I fumbled to reach the nightstand. Straining to sound as if I was wide-awake, I spoke a hearty "Hello."

The long-distance operator said, "I have a call for Mister Bob Alberti from Chicago." In the early 1950s calls were still placed through operators.

"That's me," I answered. Chicago? I didn't think I knew anyone from Chicago

A rather raspy voice on the other end said, "How'd ya like to go for a ride in a Cadillac?"

Before I could fathom what I'd heard and finish saying, "Who is this?", the voice continued... "....in the trunk! Lay off the broad!" There was the ominous click of the other party hanging up. Then came a momentary pause in my breathing, as I tried to comprehend what I'd just heard. It dawned on me that the hatcheck girl in the mafia-run club where I was playing had a closer connection to the boss than I had been aware of, and this was my first warning. I didn't need a second one. After having a cigarette, I pondered how this sort of situation could happen to a nice nineteen-year old kid in Brooklyn who just wanted to play jazz piano, and have an occasional liaison with a comely young lady. I couldn't get back to sleep the rest of that night. I avoided any contact with the lady in question from that time forward.

Having been raised in Brooklyn, survival skills were paramount. As an eight—year old, my greatest desire was to live to be nine. When warning signs became obvious, I learned to take the best way out. Dropping this nightclub romance fit that pattern precisely. To much of the world, Brooklyn has a negative connotation. The convoluted dialect that became known as *Brooklynese* was not relegated to that borough alone. It was prevalent in the greater New York/New Jersey area, the by-product of kids whose parents had emigrated from Europe. These youngsters learned the language in the street, with no guidance from within their respective homes. Not all Brooklynites had that patois; I was born in to a family of fourth generation upstate New Yorkers whose greeting was more of a "Howdy" than the usual grunted "Hey". My grandfather was from Central Square, just outside Syracuse. Grandmother was from Buffalo, and most of the relatives on my maternal side still resided in the upper reaches of New York State.

Single-family homes lined the streets of Bay Ridge, a fairly new neighborhood in Brooklyn at the time, with many of them overlooking a body of water known as "The Narrows." The majestic ocean liners of the 1930s would pass through this inlet enroute to and from their trans-Atlantic voyages. The residents were predominantly Scandinavian, Italian, Irish, Jewish and Syrian, most of who were immigrants of the early 20th century. Somehow, we seemed to all get along with few skirmishes. Brooklyn had trees. Brooklyn had gangs. Brooklyn also had pianos, many pianos. They were a focal point of home entertainment and most hadn't been tuned in recent memory. Luckily for me, the first one I can recall from early childhood was tuned with regularity. The black Conway grand piano that sat in our living room in Bay Ridge had a profound influence on my path in life. It is said that young people exposed to music at a very early age will tend to remember musical pitch more than those who have had no close musical association. In later life this would enter into play with my career choice.

Dysfunctional families were as prevalent back in the '30s as they are today. The only difference is that in the earlier times, a label hadn't been attached to describe the syndrome. Mine was right in keeping with the trend, a bunch of unhappy wackos. The union, brief as it may have been of thirty-one year old itinerant bandleader Julian Robert Alberti (a.k.a. Jules) my father, and eighteen-year-old pseudo-princess Marjorie Kendall Tebeau, my mother produced their only son, Robert Lewis Alberti. I was born in the early morning hours of December 1st, 1934. Jules was a silver-tongued smoothie, who unbeknownst to Marjorie had been married three times prior, starting with his first elopement at age fifteen. His reputation as a ladies man was far reaching among his associates, and his charms managed to be seductive to a number of comely lasses, although my mother didn't know this at the time. The process of my entering the world as a human being was not all that serene. There were no gynecologists in the early 1930s, so the attending physician was our family doctor, Morris Rosen. His knowledge of the birthing process was one step below that of a midwife, and from what I was told in later years, my coming into the world tore up my mother's reproductive system to the point where she could never again conceive. I personally doubt that she had any desire to do so a second time, but this was one of the events in her life that she would occasionally hold out as a weapon, assumedly to make me feel guilty about being born. While my mother was experiencing my difficult birth at Victory Memorial Hospital, the night was shattered by the sound of a patient in the next room, who had a brain infection. He suddenly went berserk and trashed his hospital quarters, had to be restrained, and died while being forced into a straight jacket. My mother witnessed all of this. How much of a traumatic effect this may have had on her isn't known, but throughout my early years my grandmother often related that incident to me. Shortly after that, mother began a lifelong romance with alcohol that eventually would lead to an estrangement from those closest to her. This was the "flapper" era, and young women were beginning to assert their independence while trying to break away from their parents'

Victorian mold. The premature role of motherhood could very likely have been an added reason Marjorie escaped into the alcoholic abyss.

Jules and Marjorie divorced shortly after I arrived on the scene. Home as I grew to know it was with my maternal grandparents. With me in tow, Marjorie went back to live with them. They may or may not have been glad to see another generation enter their domicile. Her dad, Lewis Perry Tebeau had married Sigournee Kendall (known familiarly as "Gurnee,") on her rebound from a suitor's rejection. They were remnants of the Victorian era, having been raised in the Buffalo/Toronto area. I wouldn't have labeled them "bumpkins," but certainly they were less than sophisticated, and definitely not at all in love. Throughout the sixteen years I lived in their home, I never heard a loving remark or saw a friendly gesture from either one to the other.

My mother Marjorie, the younger of two siblings was the "golden girl" of her parents' eyes. She learned at a very young age how to manipulate them, and continued to do so well into her adulthood. She seemingly always got her way, with threats and tantrums, much to the displeasure of her parents and her brother. According to family legend, her parents slept together twice, each time producing an offspring. The first was Robert Lewis Tebeau, known to me as "Uncle Bob." The next one along the way was four years later, when Marjorie was born. From that time forward, father & son slept in one bedroom, mother & daughter in the other. There were no signs of wear on the carpet connecting the two rooms. When I arrived, the crib went in with the ladies and there I stayed until Uncle Bob married and moved out. That was the signal to move in with Grandpa Tebeau. Sharing a double bed with this somewhat portly gentleman was not a thrill for an eleven-year-old lad, but I was informed that I had no choice at the time. Despite my requests for my own bed, I had to share the one that my uncle had slept in along with grandpa for years. The mattress sagged on gramps' side since he was by far the heavier of the two of us. A lucky dream one night had me lost in the woods, searching desperately for a restroom, where I could relieve myself. I settled on the trunk of an oak tree, which in reality happened to be my grandfather's back. Shortly after that the old double bed was replaced with twins. Who says dreams don't come true!

I was raised, for the most part by my grandparents. My mother at eighteen was a very emotionally immature woman, a characteristic that stayed with her throughout her entire life. The desire to perform and be noticed was an integral part of her early personality. Having taken dancing lessons as a young girl, she found work as a dancer in a chorus line with a traveling troupe, which is how she managed to meet my father. She had done bits in Olsen & Johnson's "Hellzapoppin'," and had been an extra in one of D. W. Griffith's early films. That movie was shot at a film studio in downtown Brooklyn in the early '30s, and her desire to be in show business was no secret. Her show-biz career, brief as it was, led her to adopt a stage name: Jerri Joyce. All her luggage had the initials J.J. emblazoned on them, and naturally my childish curiosity piqued when I realized that there wasn't anyone I knew in our family with that monogram. She was not ready to settle into motherhood at age eighteen, and left town to work in Florida at the Hollywood Beach Hotel as an Arthur Murray dance instructor. Until the age of about five, I was raised by my grandparents in Brooklyn, with two short trips to Florida to visit my high-steppin' momma, who by this time had pretty well mastered the art of downing whatever sort of whiskey was near at hand. At about six years of age, I found my wandering mother moving back in the Brooklyn domicile with her parents. This led to a myriad of conflicts between my mother who had been absent and my grandmother who raised me as a surrogate. Marjorie was an ultimate control freak and insisted that whatever I'd been taught was incorrect by her standards. Ultimately, her return into my life at that stage was not something I welcomed. She eventually took a nine-to-five job in Manhattan that got her off my back eight hours a day. Trying to deal with an alcoholic parent is never easy and my early relationship with my mother was no exception.

My father had moved to nearby New Jersey, to avoid

having to come up with the $7.00 weekly child support the New York divorce court decreed that he pay. He had always lived by his wits, keeping one step ahead of the creditors, and although his outward appearance was that of a successful gentleman, the tailor who made his suits was after him for money owed, as was his landlord at the Parc Vendome apartments on West 57th Street in Manhattan for back rent. He always had big plans but they never seemed to materialize. As I matured into my teenage years I resented him for my sense of abandonment, even more so for all the promises of what he would do for my career, none of which ever came to fruition. This eventually caused a long-term estrangement between us that wasn't resolved until I was informed in 1976 that he was on his deathbed. Shortly after he and my mother had divorced, he found wife number five, singer Maybelle Ross. Maybelle was one of three sisters who sang as a trio, aptly named "DO-RE-MI." She was the type of woman who chose to act as a surrogate mother to Jules, which I suspect is what he was searching for and didn't find with the four previous attempts at matrimony. That union lasted until his death. Unbeknownst to Maybelle, Dad had a continuing romance going with his manicurist for about twenty years, and that relationship didn't come to light until his death.

Dad was quite a handsome man, albeit short of stature. He had a number of career twists and turns, which were generally glamorous and very visible. When he and mother met, he was the leader of a twelve-piece dance band. He wore a white bow tie, carried the baton with dignity, and always had a winning smile. Somewhere along the way, something occurred that brought his musical career to an end. I heard two sides to the story. Mother claimed he was expelled from the musicians union for taking kickbacks. Dad claimed that his band beat out a Chicago band led by Caesar Petrillo, nephew of union boss James C. Petrillo in an audition. Dad held fast that the charges were trumped up by the elder Petrillo to clear the way for his nephew's career surge. I'll never know the truth.

Later on, he was approached by someone he had met in his years as a bandleader, and was asked to head the celebrity coordination in the war bond drive during World War II. He worked hard finding well-known performers to appear at rallies to sell bonds for the duration of the war, and as a result befriended many famous singers and actors. This led to his next career change. Dad managed to wheedle himself into a position of personal manager to actress Constance Bennett, who would be known as "Aunt Connie" to me. She was under contract to 20th Century Fox Studios in Hollywood, and it meant that dad would have to fly coast-to-coast on numerous occasions. He reveled in the aura of Hollywood, which was fine while it lasted; however, he was in the southern California area when a large earthquake shook the landscape. It petrified him to such a degree that he quit his managerial position and refused from that day forward to ever set foot in California again.

The connections he made in his war bond years led him to another scheme. He started an agency called "Endorsements, Inc." which was touted to advertisers as a sure way to pair the correct celebrity with a particular product. This was at a time when Madison Avenue ad executives were realizing that celebrity endorsements could sell products, and Dad had gotten a lot of name personalities to sign exclusive agreements allowing him to be their middleman. Every time an ad agency needed a well-known personality to be on a billboard or a Wheaties box, Jules Alberti and Endorsements, Inc. were called upon. The business prospered for a time, but eventually the major ad agencies opened their own in-house divisions, and his business was relegated to a one-room office in an aging building on West 57th Street in Manhattan. This was the business in which he remained for the rest of his life.

Back to the living room piano. It was always there, always tuned, and occasionally played by my mother (to a degree) after she returned home after her years of gadding about in Florida. She had a decent musical ear and a fairly good rhythmic sense. She could read simple sheet music and was a devotee of the swing era, which in 1939 was in its heyday. Uncle Bob would do likewise but in a more methodical manner since he was a statistician. His mindset was to analyze before acting upon anything and that tended to slow down his attempts at playing music. He'd try and figure things out as he played, searching for the notes that sounded best for what he was attempting. Spontaneity was not in any way a part of his personality. Grandma Gurnee would occasionally sit on the bench and try to read from simple songbooks, her head alternately tilting up and down to accommodate her bifocals, looking first at the music, then down at the keyboard. Grandpa Tebeau was completely tone deaf, playing nothing and unable to differentiate between a trumpet and a cello.

Uncle Bob had a nurturing propensity toward me. When I was a lad of four or five, he would spend a great deal of time with me, taking me to the Brooklyn Museum to hear the Brooklyn Symphony play Sunday afternoon concerts by the masters. He also taught me the names of the various notes on the piano keyboard. This would eventually lead to the discovery that I had perfect pitch, which came about when he was ponderously searching for the correct bass note to some selection he was trying to play. I was in the bedroom, a good twenty feet away from the living room. I guess I was no more than five years of age at the time, and I listened to the sounds emanating from the piano. I yelled to him, "Unk, if you play an "F" in the bottom instead of a "G" it'll sound better!" He did, as if it had been a matter of fact, and it worked. About ten seconds later, he did a double take and stopped playing. He called back, "How did you know I was playing a 'G'?" I had no rational answer....I thought everybody knew that particular sound was a 'G'. He then began to test me by hitting different notes and having me identify them. That was easy. Then he tried two notes at a time, also easy. Then triads and clusters, and I identified them all. This brought about a revelation to him and the family. In their naiveté, the word "genius" was liberally bantered about to describe me. An exaggeration to be sure, but I guess it made them feel special in some peculiar way. I wasn't sure what it all meant, but I assumed that it was some sort of advantage for me.

Then came a succession of local piano teachers, all of whom I hated! My ears were attuned to swing and jazz, not "In A

Country Garden," or "Humoresque." I cried, yelled and tossed one tantrum after another, rebelling against the methodology of teaching piano of that era. None of the teachers lasted more than about three weeks. Finally, they would throw up their hands and resign in frustration. My mother was somewhat relieved. She didn't want me to become a musician anyway, since her brief connection with my father had soured her on musicians in general. As I think back, I chose a career in music as one way to spite her. She was not an easy person to go up against, since she could be extremely volatile after the third martini, which was usually about 2:00 in the afternoon. This was one way I could control some portion of my independence from her.

I made many adjustments in my life as a Brooklyn boy, and learned survival by staying off the streets and immersing myself in the one obvious talent I had, which was music. In the long run, it paid off.

As a side note to my reconciliation with my father, in 1976 he informed me as he lay on his death-bed in a New York hospital, that I had a half-sister who was nine months younger than me. My paternal grandmother Rose Alberti had run a rooming house in Chicago, and after Dad's divorce from my mother that was the location where he retreated. Dad certainly didn't spend a lot of time having his mama console him. During his brief visit to her domicile, he immediately befriended a single gal who had a room at this mother's establishment. He managed to ply his charms on this particular lady, who then left the rooming house never to see Dad again, never to let him know that she was pregnant with his child. The baby, as it turned out was named Marjorie, the same as my mother. Whether this was some sort of cruel joke or simply a coincidence will never be known. Years later, sister Marjorie set out on a quest to seek out her father after finding that her mother had lied to her, by telling her that her father was dead. Marj, as I've come to know her is a delightful lady who seems to share a number of genetic characteristics with me. As I go through life, I have trepidations that I may continue to meet some more half-siblings, all of whom may have the Jules Alberti charm characteristics. This part of his personality managed to pass me by since I've always tended to be more of an anti-social loner, although many of the other Alberti genes were bestowed upon me. Some were totally omitted including the sportsman's gene. My father and I were very similar in our inability to catch or throw a ball in any desired direction. The "football gene" was completely absent. Fishing was a wipeout in my eyes, which was a big disappointment to my grandfather Tebeau, whose only joy in life was rummaging through his tackle box, eagerly anticipating his next annual weeklong venture into the lakes of Canada. Undeniably, the genetic memory for music was omnipresent, and it came from the great-grandparents on the Alberti side. Great-grandpa Samuel Alberti migrated to America from Castellamare, Italy with wife and five kids in tow, as the Alberti Family Orchestra. His son Louis became a violinist, then later conductor at the Chicago Theatre. Another son, Solon became an operatic vocal coach in New York City. Grandson Julian (my dad) had a dance band in the 1930s that broadcast on CBS with regularity. I was predestined to follow music as my pathway through life. It was a natural way to go, since I never had a tendency to enter into local athletic or group activities. As I look back, I couldn't have asked for better genes! They would eventually shape my very existence, and would last throughout my entire life.

CHAPTER 2

ADOLESCENCE

If you happen to be a bit chubby, non-athletic and acne-ridden when you approach puberty, any escape that you can find will provide a safe haven for moments of angst. The piano proved to be such an object for my salvation. Although I was usually able to exert control over what my fingers did on a keyboard, the rest of my body suffered (and still does) from a form of clumsiness. I couldn't judge a fly ball and saw many land thirty feet away from me while all the time yelling, "I got it!" When I was fortunate enough to almost come in contact with a baseball, it would never find the pocket of my glove. It would skip off the end of a finger leaving me with a sprain that would take a week or more to heal. I had terrible balance, and couldn't even so much as stand on roller skates. I realized early on that the only way I was going to survive in the outside world was on the strength of my musical ability.

Being of an aesthetic rather than athletic nature, social situations were generally elusive. Dating in my early teen years was almost non-existent, and I compensated in my high school days by taking every music course I could. Band, orchestra, instrument practice and music theory took the place of shop, phys-ed, and more scholastic courses that I would have needed to get an academic diploma. I failed miserably in math, having to repeat algebra one for two consecutive terms. I never did grasp it and was told that the best I could do would be to aim for a General Diploma, which meant that I'd attended school for the time required by law. More and more it became apparent that music was to be my livelihood as academia and I drifted further apart.

Somehow I ended up being one year younger than most of my classmates, and in teen years, that's a considerable difference. I had just turned thirteen when I entered high school and had passed seventeen by one month when I got out. However, during those years I began to form friendships with other students in higher grades who played instruments usable in dance bands. In 1949 I formed my first five-piece band, using stock orchestrations that were available for about seventy-five cents. Our first engagement was for a dance at a local church, playing for two hours after a basketball game. We got ten dollars for the entire group, which when divided became two bucks apiece. That was barely enough for the pizza we shared after the job had concluded, but the experience was priceless.

As the weeks went on, we obtained more stock arrangements, practiced more in the living room of my grandparents' home, and got more jobs. As we would perform, I'd envy my classmates on the dance floor, grinding bodies with the cheerleaders and doing fancy dips. I was jealous since I couldn't make my feet correlate with any other body part, so I saw my music as the only spotlight I could bring upon myself. I guess at this point my ego became entwined with my pianistic abilities. It became increasingly apparent that certain genes were absent in my genome map; the athletic gene, and the body-coordination gene were two that spring to mind.

During my days in high school, I studied a different instrument each term as an extra class in instrument practice. I learned and became fairly proficient on the clarinet and alto saxophone, decent enough to play the occasional club date with someone else's band that already had a pianist. I didn't do quite as well on trumpet and string bass but enough to know the capabilities and registers of each instrument and how they functioned as non-concert pitch instruments. This became invaluable in due course as I proceeded to teach myself music orchestrating and arranging.

With the encouragement of my high school music teacher David Rattner, I embarked on writing small arrangements for tenor bands that were still popular in hotels and restaurants. Although I was a poor reader of piano music, I could easily figure out single-stave parts. The bands consisted of three tenor saxophones, one or two trumpets and a rhythm section. I wrote about ten charts that I proceeded to advertise in Down Beat Magazine, a journal for the music trade. I had a few orders, and since Xerox hadn't come up with a decent copier at that time, I'd go to a blueprint house to have the parts duplicated. This produced white notes and white staves on blue backgrounds, which were far from easy to read. Since I never had a tenor band I really didn't know how these charts sounded except in my mind. For all I knew there could have been a dozen notation errors in any given chart, but it was my entrée into the world of arranging which would eventually become a major part of my career.

At age fifteen, I had a five-piece group consisting of piano, bass, drums guitar and tenor sax playing every weekend at Foffe's restaurant in Brooklyn. The child labor laws weren't very strict at that time and since some of the players in my band were in their twenties, nobody questioned my boyish appearance. We also played at the Officer's Club at Fort Hamilton as well as the N.C.O. club at the same nearby army base. A Veterans of Foreign Wars post was another spot for an evening of dining, dancing and fighting. This was Brooklyn after all. I realized in another year I'd be free of the bondage of school and my mind was made up. I was going to make my living in the world of music.

The bassist in my band was a lad named Lou Cordaro, who had almost perfect pitch and a great ear for finding the proper bass notes for each song. His cousin Sal Cordaro was a "ringer," since Sal was twenty-three and long out of high school. Sal played electric guitar in a style modeled after his idol, Chuck Wayne. Sal was also a bit vague, and somewhat spacey. One night after finishing a job at a Veterans of Foreign Wars post, the band members headed to a pizzeria. En route, Sal mentioned that he must have been getting stronger since his guitar case felt very light. Upon closer examination, he found the reason:

He'd left his guitar at the gig site and walked out with an empty case. Saxophonist Walter Hermann and drummer Ray Filfiley rounded out the group.

Since we had summers off from school, the Catskill Mountains had great lure for us kids. It was a way to play in a band all summer, meet girls and get out of the oppressive heat in New York City. I spent seven summers at various hotels learning my trade at the expense of a lot of singers and other artists. Since I was mainly a self-taught "ear-player," my reading skills were close to non-existent. This didn't sit well with some of the old-time acts whose music had been around the world for fifty years and was dog-eared and yellowed with age. There were so many markings on the parts that one could barely make out the notes, not that it would have made that much difference. I probably wouldn't have been able to read them even if they'd been legible. I could read them one note at a time and maybe put something together eventually. However, we'd have a fifteen-minute rehearsal for each act since most of them played three different hotels each night. They had to rehearse with the band at each hotel, then take their music and go to the next hotel. This meant I didn't have an opportunity to psych out the parts after rehearsal. The music would later come back to me having been marked up by two other piano players that afternoon, and by then it looked like something I'd never laid eyes on.

Word spread quickly as to my musical strengths and weaknesses in New York, and before long I was known as "Good ears, can't read." Once a musician gets pigeonholed in New York, it takes many years for that categorization to be forgotten. The "can't read" stigma would stay with me for years to come, even though I worked diligently to learn how to read music, and eventually I became proficient enough to be an accomplished studio pianist in Los Angeles whose ultimate reputation was "Can read anything." In New York, however, the negative reputation remained.

I encountered a number of famous performers on their way up or down in the world of show biz. Some were nice, understanding people. Most, however, tended to be very egocentric and short on patience with younger musicians. One notable female singer who is about my age, give or take a couple of months, was acting a prima donna at one of the Catskill resort rehearsals. After taking as much as I could, I stopped playing, and shouted,

"Listen! I've loused up a lot better singers than you. Just do your job! I'll do mine as best as I can, and maybe we'll survive without coming to blows!"

We managed to get through it. As fate would have it, about thirty years later that artist would come to Hollywood and land a part in a prime time series playing a singer. When asked if there was a pianist she would prefer, her answer was, "Yes. The only pianist who told me off and got away with it!" We spent two seasons as friends on the series. I speak of the lovely and talented Diahann Carroll.

Throughout this era of my life I was dealing with incessant acne. My ultimate fear was that I'd become one huge pustule that would eventually explode. I suppose that wasn't unusual for someone in his late teens, but my self-image was suffering with the pimples and blotches that are a part of adolescence. Back then every barbershop touted ultra-violet treatments as a cure for the problem. The only result I achieved from baking every month for twenty minutes under an ultra violet lamp was a plethora of basal cell carcinomas in later years. I had to come to terms that I wasn't a "Don Juan" and for certain, I never would be. The pimples remained and I continued to focus on the one strong point I knew, my natural musical ability.

First Band, 1949
Left to Right: Ray Filfiley (drums), Tom McKenny (alto & clarinet),
Frank Bianco (tenor), Jay Compton (trumpet), Bob (piano)

Foffe's Restaurant
Brooklyn, NY, 1950
Left to Right: Bob (piano), Lou Cordaro (bass), Walter
Hermann (tenor), Sal Cordaro (guitar), Ray Filfiley (drums).

CHAPTER 3

THE UNION

Union: A word that had been bandied about as long as I could recall. The story of my father's exit from the union has yet to be proven true or false, but as it was relayed to me, the union, the specter of an all-powerful organization that could make or break one's career was something of which to be in awe. In major cities such as New York one could not find any decent paying work without a union card. The union was something to be desired, and yet feared at the same time. This was especially true to a fifteen-year-old "wannabee" musician.

In order to work around New York back in the early 1950s, one **had** to be a union member. Union delegates (a.k.a."goons") would be sent to the nightclubs and bars where live music was being played, and they'd ask to see your paid-up union card. Without one, they'd pull all the players out, so if you were a non-member, union bands wouldn't hire you.

One day, along with a couple of my high school musician buddies, I boarded the subway to the headquarters of Local 802, which at the time was located downtown on Houston Street. The offices were upstairs, and the ground level was what was known as the union floor. Every Monday, Wednesday and Friday hundreds of musicians would gather to make contact with the various club date contractors. Lester Lanin, Mark Towers, Meyer Davis, and all the other society leaders had numerous bands out almost every night of the week. They each

had a contractor, a specific person, usually a musician who would
do the hiring and make certain that each band had the correct
number of bodies and instruments. Musicians would circulate
from one contractor to another seeking work. Likewise, if
the contractor spotted a musician he knew and wanted, he'd
approach him asking something like, "Ya got Saturday night?"
The musician would take his little pocket diary out of his
back pocket, thumb through it and either say, "Sorry...I'm
booked." Or, he'd try to wheedle extra dates, by only taking the
Saturday night if the contractor tossed in a Sunday afternoon
or a weeknight as well. Most all the big events were planned
on Saturdays, so in order to make a decent living, one would
bargain for additional dates.

At the time I was totally new to this sort of procedure, and
was quite nervous knowing that I had to take a test in order to
get into the union. I was directed to the membership office,
and had to fill out the usual admission papers. Then I was told
to sit outside in a little room and wait for my name to be called.
Being barely fifteen, this whole thing seemed overwhelming.
Knowing I was somewhere between a lousy music reader and a
non music reader, I had a feeling of dread come over me while
in that waiting room. Was it going to be Chopin or Bach that
they'd toss in front of me? The minutes seemed to go on forever
while my palms grew sweatier.

Then the moment came. The door to an enclosed cubicle
opened and a portly old gent in a white shirt with his sleeves
rolled up said, "Alberti?" With my rigid body almost frozen with
fear, I managed to stand, walk and enter the room. Inside was
an old upright piano with no visible music anywhere around. He
looked over my paperwork, and said "Sit down at the piano." I
did so.

"Play an F-sharp chord."

I did.

"Now play a G-flat chord."

I did.

"Aha! Can't fool you. You're in. Go over to the window and
pay your fifty bucks. They'll give your card!"

Anyone who has the slightest semblance of musical knowledge knows that an F sharp and a G flat chord are one in the same. My nervousness was all for naught. As I was breathing normally once more, paying my initiation fee, the door opened again and the tester yelled, "Alberti! Come back here." Once again, I froze. Nonetheless I headed back, wondering what lay in store. He asked if I knew any current tunes, and I nodded affirmatively. He asked me to play one, so I sat down and played a chorus of "Talk of the Town," a song popular at that time. He then asked if I'd be interested in playing a weekend in the Catskill Mountains. He'd just given a test to a clarinetist who'd recently won the Paul Whiteman talent award, with his rendition of " Rhapsody in Blue." The hotel, something just short of a *cochalane was* obviously not interested in paying big bucks, and had called the union to see if they could furnish a "kid band" for some weekend of Jewish holidays. For those who have never shared the experience, a *cochalane* is a Yiddish word denoting a house and bungalow colony, usually with a shared kitchen.

At this point, I was introduced to a lanky kid, probably no more than sixteen by the name of Owen Engel. He was to be the leader for the weekend, and along with him came a drummer who had minimal skills, and no ability to keep time. However, he was eighteen, had a car and a drivers license, and for that alone, became a needed commodity. Engel's claim to fame was having won a Paul Whiteman talent contest with his rendition of "Rhapsody In Blue" on the clarinet, a selection that he would end with the clarinet pointing skyward with a flourish.

After a two-hour ride up route seventeen, we arrived at the *Golden Hotel and Cottages*, an old hotel in the Catskill Mountains. The average age of the residents was somewhere between elderly and deceased. Their requests for eastern European dances such as horas and frailachs were not at all familiar to this *goy*, (another Yiddish term for *Gentile)* and apparently not even to Mr. Engel, who happened to be Jewish. I found out that all he could play was "Rhapsody in Blue". That was the extent of his repertoire. At least I knew about 40 or 50 pop tunes, so between the drummer and me, we managed to provide some recognizable tunes to the portion of the audience who had a smattering of hearing left. I think we made $40 apiece for the three-day weekend, and it seemed pretty good for a fifteen-year-old kid to feel some sense of independence. Union scale wages for the first time at age fifteen!

Union! Hot damn!

CHAPTER 4

INTO THE REAL WORLD

I knew that upon completing four years of sitting in high school daydreaming, sooner or later I'd have to think about earning some hard cash. I was seventeen at the end of the Truman era, entering into the naïve Eisenhower years. This was not pop music's finest hour, as novelty tunes were flooding the market. "Sing Along with Mitch" was a T.V. staple, and the Doris Day era was in full swing. The mood was set by the record moguls, the omnipotent A & R men, whose job it was to try to sense what the public wanted to hear. I don't think the public wanted to hear much of the slop that was being chosen to record, but nonetheless, if one's hungry, the best of the worst will be devoured. Novelty songs abounded as the likes of Cole Porter and Richard Rodgers waned.

My desire to be in the music business full time was always there. However, when the day came for me to be presented with my "General Diploma," I had some decisions to make. My grandparents had hinted that if I wanted to remain living at home I'd have to start contributing to the household finances. This set me looking over the local want ads for anything that would make me into a productive adult and allow me to save some money to put toward my future independence. I definitely wanted to move out from under the aging and gloomy household of my grandparents. By this time my mother had once again married and divorced after one year from a 60-year-old Italian urologist, who until they wed had lived at home

with his mother as a bachelor. My mother's inability to keep
him from playing the ponies was one part of the breakup. Her
inability to make pasta sauce like his momma made was another,
and she proceeded to delve deeper into the vodka bottle. In any
event, she chose to go on living independently after the divorce
and stayed in Manhattan. I was still in Brooklyn by choice, not
wanting to have much to do with her, and definitely not wanting
to be around the doctor. He was an Italian version of the guy
in the painting, "American Gothic." Not exactly a bundle of
laughs.

My first stab at employment was selling Electrolux
vacuums door-to-door. That lasted about a week, since I have
no sales savvy. I always rang the doorbell with an attitude that
revealed, "You probably don't want one of these things anyway."
I was right. Nobody did, and after a week I gave up the venture.
Back to the want ads.

My second try in the real world was as an office boy in
the insurance offices of Crum & Forster down in the Wall
Street area of Manhattan. The pay was $37.50 a week, and that
wasn't too bad if I brought my own lunch. Carfare was still a
dime on the subway, so I could toss $10 a week into the home
food kitty and have enough for a beer or two or an occasional
date. However, by the third day I realized I hated the office
atmosphere, and also the two other mailroom gavonnes with
whom I had to work. I handed in my notice, which took me to
the end of week number two. I was now a former employee.

As a young musician I had learned that a great portion of
musical knowledge came via osmosis. Hanging around where
music was being played was a great way to hear sounds that were
happening, and one of the places to go for such an experience
was Nola Studios. Nola occupied an entire floor on Broadway
and 50th Street, and most of the name bands that were still in
existence would regularly rehearse there. The central lobby was
surrounded with rehearsal rooms and one recording studio. I
was only one of the young hopefuls who would sneak into the
rehearsal rooms to hear bands like the Dorseys, Neal Hefti, and
others who happened to be in town. One day I was listening to

bandleader Charlie Spivak go over a bunch of new arrangements written by Manny Albam. They were mostly standard tunes that I'd heard and played at some point in time. As luck would have it the piano chair was empty, and during one of the breaks, a ruddy-faced alto saxophonist named Charlie Russo approached me. He asked what I was doing there, and I explained that I was a pianist and was simply listening.

"Do you wanna sit in, kid?" he asked.

I felt my nerves starting to kick in. In times of stress my hands would become icy cold, my face would flush and I'd feel as if a fast trip to the nearest bathroom was a necessity. All these factors came into play when I realized that I'd be in a famous orchestra with seasoned musicians of legendary reputations. As if I were being guided by a power beyond my control, I put on a face of the most self-assured bravado and agreed to attempt the role of band pianist.

They ran down a few tunes and I tried my best to follow the hand-scripted chord charts that to me at the time resembled hieroglyphics. Reading music was not my strong point since I was essentially an ear-player, and had gotten by as such to this point. Having perfect pitch, I could automatically tell in what key the arrangement was written, and whenever it modulated I'd go right along with it. If nobody else was playing except the drums and bass, I assumed it was a piano solo, so I'd fudge my way through the eight or sixteen bars. After a few tunes the band took a break.

I was still shaking with nervous exhilaration over the experience I had just gone through when Charlie Russo came over with Spivak, who introduced himself to me. At that point, Russo said,

"We need a piano player kid. Would you like to join up?"

I didn't know what to say, so I stammered a bit.

"Pays a hundred an' forty a week," he added.

Hearing that dollar figure, I accepted without hesitation.

A hundred and forty dollars a week! Man! I knew my grandfather had been working as a clerk at a brokerage office for thirty years and was only pulling down sixty-five dollars per week. I was actually going to get more than double what he made...and at age seventeen!

As I arrived home I told my grandmother what I was about to do, which sent her into one of her predictable nervous tizzies. I immediately went out to buy a suitcase. It was a hard-shelled Samsonite in blue with a white border, almost the size of a steamer trunk. It was all I could do to lift it when it was empty, and I never considered the consequences when it was loaded for a two-week road trip.

I was informed the Spivak band would depart from the President Hotel on West 48th Street. The band bus would load from there and head off to Pittsburgh for the first of many one-nighters. I was truly the "kid" in the band, while the other band members were hardened road-rats who'd been doing this for a good long while. Who better to learn from than guys like this? It seemed as though the President Hotel was the stopping point for most all the bands of the day when they were in New York. At seven dollars a night and with two guys sharing a room, it was a decent deal. I got to know players from the Tex Beneke band, as well as those from Sam Donahue, Tommy Dorsey and other ensembles of the now fading big-band era. It was there I first met Lynn Roberts, the vocalist with the Dorsey band, who at the time was dating Daryl "Flea" Campbell, the lead trumpeter with the Spivak band. They later married and divorced, but they have remained close friends with one another and to this day I stay in touch with both of them. Eydie Gorme was the band vocalist for Tex Beneke and we'd occasionally pass in the lobby of the President Hotel.

As in every era, there were big-band groupies who would do anything to be associated with the musicians that were respected and admired in the '40s and '50s. The most notorious was a woman dubbed "Mattress Annie" by the dozens of musicians for whom she provided sexual gratification. Her true first name was Pat, and she was a denizen of the two hotels in midtown that housed traveling bands, the aforementioned President and The Forrest Hotel one block away. Pat had unkempt blond hair and was slightly cross-eyed. Whenever possible, she would stow away in the luggage compartment of a band bus while it was being loaded, and ultimately be discovered when the band got to the first venue of a two-week road trip. By this time it was too late and too costly to ship her back to the city, so she took turns sharing the bedrooms of some of the hornier musicians. As an inexperienced seventeen-year-old, I was fearful of whatever disease she may have had. I also found her less than attractive, so I kept my hotel room door locked at all times. In retrospect, I may be one of a very small elite circle who chose not to partake of what this woman had to offer.

The one common thread among most of the players was their ability to consume outrageous amounts of alcohol with some starting at eight o'clock in the morning, the legal time for the bars to open. For a while, I attempted to join those ranks, but my gastric system precluded me from matching drink for drink with the more experienced guys. Once I tried beginning a road trip with three rye and ginger ales in lieu of breakfast. Throughout that whole trip to Boston I had my head out the bus window, barfing up my substitute breakfast plus whatever was still in my digestive tract from the night before. I soon gave up the quest to be a seasoned elbow-bender.

For almost a year of one-nighters, I boarded the bus that was rented from the Flying Eagle White Lines, an old diesel job with no rest room on board. To relieve oneself, one would have to stand in the entry stairwell of the bus and have the driver open the door slightly. Another band member would hold you by the back of your trousers and belt while you unzipped and proceeded to urinate as the bus kept rolling along the highway. To make matters worse, the girl singer occupied the front seat by the door, and we never knew whether she was really asleep or had one eye cracked open. I couldn't quite figured out how she handled this function while rolling down the highway.

Our "band chirp" as female singers were called back then was from Pittsburgh. Her nickname was "Max" since she had a habit of smoking cigars. It may be fashionable for women to do so in the 21st century, but in the 1950s it was considered a bit bizarre. She was a decent belter of songs but was very gullible and was the butt of many put-ons. She would innocently ask questions such as, "Is the Pacific Ocean on the West Coast?" This left the door open for smart-asses such as myself to create situations that would laughingly be recounted years later.

One night while the band was at the Café Rouge of the Hotel Statler in New York, we were on a break. We'd sit in the raised wings, which were only opened and used for full houses or special events. The Café Rouge served everything flambéed on carts with little cans of Sterno, keeping the skillets sizzling. At the time I was a cigarette smoker, so while sitting at one of the tables with Max, I lit a cigarette and proceeded to toss the match into the open can of Sterno. Anyone who has camped out knows that it has the substance of a red jelly. It began to burn.

Max looked at it for a moment, and asked, "What's that stuff?"

"It's Jello...Whaddeya think it was?" I answered facetiously.

"Does all Jello burn like that?" she asked.

"Naw...Only the raspberry."

"Oh."

That seemed to quell her thirst for knowledge, and life went on.

The Spivak band was the first taste I'd had of the world of professional orchestras. The era of big bands was rapidly winding down, and the few remaining orchestras didn't have enough steady work to hire musicians on a full-time basis. There would be an occasional weekend in the New York area, or four nights in the Midwest, or if one was lucky, a ballroom gig. I was lucky enough to get hired by Don Rodney, whose only claim to fame was his stint as a guitarist and singer with the Guy Lombardo band. Rodney, whose real surname was Ragonese, had the dance band at the Arcadia Ballroom on 53rd Street and Broadway. Although the band was not great, it at least allowed me to remain in New York while earning a decent living. Nepotism prevailed as he had his nephew purportedly playing bass, and lead-footed former Glenn Miller drummer Maurice ("Moe") Purtill comprising the remainder of the rhythm section. It never swung. It couldn't swing if it tried. It was like trying to run the mile with shackles on. I played there for a few months and during an off time, Rodney was booked into the Palisades Amusement Park in New Jersey. It was April of '53, and the temperature was about 40 degrees. We were in an outdoor pavilion and the rains came. The park emptied rapidly, and those of us on the bandstand were freezing. The park boss, a hardheaded nudnik, insisted that we play until the contractual closing time. My fingers were turning blue prompting me to remember that I had fur-lined gloves in my car. On the first break I got them from the old Plymouth in the parking area, resumed my place on the bandstand and began to play with the gloves on. The outer layer was heavy leather, and each finger was about twice as wide as a normal finger would be. Each single note I hit became a cluster, and at this point I didn't really give a damn. I'd had it with Don Rodney and company. He kept looking over, gesturing for me to remove the gloves. I kept ignoring him. His last threat was if I didn't remove them I'd be fired. I played my discords even louder. He finally yelled, "You're fired!"

I took that opportunity to get up from the piano bench, grab my overcoat and head for the car, right in the middle of a band number. I headed for home, and that was the last I saw or heard from Don Rodney. At least my hands were warm driving back to my apartment in Brooklyn.

There were numerous other bands after Don Rodney. A contractor named Hy Mandel on the union floor was the one selected to put bands together for the local leaders of diminishing name bands. I worked briefly for Jerry Gray (nee Graziano), a former arranger for Glenn Miller who put together one of the many Miller clone bands of the early 1950s. Another booking had me with Louis Prima at the Boulevard in Queens, N.Y., and also on a few road trips. This was at a time when

Prima still had a fourteen-piece organization. Keely Smith had just joined him, and they had yet to form the sextet that played for years in Las Vegas. Louis' library sounded as if some first year music school student had been handing in his homework with most charts being poorly harmonized and orchestrated. This gave me a chance to try my skills doing likewise knowing that no matter how badly I wrote, it couldn't come anywhere close to the disasters that we were already playing nightly. With the assistance of one of the alto saxophonists who knew something about arranging, I managed to get a few charts in the book.

Prima's manager, an old "Damon Runyon-esque" character by the name of Ted Eddy, had a habit of booking a lucrative tour, or so we were told. Then when we'd be in the middle of Podunk, he'd cancel the part that included the Palladium in Hollywood or the Diplomat in Miami, leaving us stranded to find our own way back to New York. After a few of these, I caught on, and when he called and asked if I wanted to go to the Sands in Las Vegas for a long term job, I sarcastically let him know that I had no intention of getting stranded in the desert and becoming coyote bait. "Take it and shove it!" I told him. Little did I know at the time that this was the one big success Prima would have and he'd hold sway there for over twenty years.

Although conditions on the road were not pleasant, the one-nighters were great learn-on-the-job experiences that unfortunately are no longer currently available to young musicians. A few "ghost bands" still remain using the arrangement libraries of deceased bandleaders, and you will usually find a majority of very young players mixed with a few lifetime "road-rats" who have never known any life other than the band bus and one-nighters. I must say I had my fill of bad food in those days. Spam and donuts were considered a two-course gourmet meal and certainly didn't help the ever-present acne.

Gradually the band business wound down enough so that I began haunting the union floor again, which by now had moved uptown into the Roseland Ballroom on West 52nd Street.

BOB ALBERTI, CHARLIE SPIVAK, DECEMBER, 1952

CHAPTER 5

THE TRAVELING YEARS

During my late teens and early twenties, I had many opportunities to see much of the country, although not in a particularly luxurious way. Most of the cars I could afford were well used and held together with chicken wire and duct tape. They did, however, manage to get me from job to job and to various cities where I'd get bookings.

One call came from a chap named Bob Tolly, a bassist of extremely limited ability who had booked a weekend in a bar in Queens, New York. This job allowed me to meet and work with guitarist Dan Fox, a highly talented and underrated jazz player. Tolly was a "rubber-band" bassist who knew very little about music, and merely snapped the strings outward so there echoed a resounding pop devoid of tonality. His talent was in singing, doing parodies and being a genial emcee. His physical presence reminded me of an emaciated Richard Widmark.

Since I seemed to fit in due to the musical simpatico I had with guitarist Dan Fox, I was offered a subsequent eight-week job in Charleston, South Carolina with the Tolly trio. This was to occur in the dead of winter so seizing the opportunity to get out of New York's frigid January and February, I gladly accepted. By this time I was about eighteen and anything south of New York City with palm trees held great appeal. I packed the oversized blue suitcase, met Dan at Pennsylvania Station and we boarded the Orange Blossom Special for Charleston.

Dan and I shared a hotel room at some old two-story

courtyard-style place in downtown Charleston. Tolly and his wife, a diminutive wisp with an ashen complexion and waist-length black hair shared a room nearby. I can't recall Mrs. Tolly's first name, but because of her bizarre and almost unearthly appearance, Dan and I referred to her as "Lady Macbeth." She was almost ghost-like in her appearance and was as strange as Bob Tolly in her demeanor. She would appear and disappear without rhyme or reason wearing a floor-length white garment. When she spoke nothing she said seemed to make much sense. Their living quarters was a hotel room at the Belleclaire Hotel on Manhattan's upper west side, where they'd been residing for years. They never cooked at home, and I have no idea what their lives were about, other than they were different from anyone I had ever met. I fantasized that she lived in a closet at that old hotel, only to be trotted out for special occasions. A perfect model for "The Addams Family."

Upon getting to the Carriage House on Market Street, our place of employment in Charleston, we met the co-owners, Izzy Sabel and Ned Dawson. These again were two types I'd never encountered in my few years of the music business. Izzy was probably about five feet two and about three hundred pounds of mostly solid muscle. His family business was the Sabel Iron & Steel Works, and I gathered that he had some connections with the southern Mafia. Ned Dawson seemed normal until he opened his mouth. At that point he may as well have been from Mars, since he spoke *Geechee,* an almost indiscernible patois of regional folk-language. Every time he'd say something to Dan or me we'd smile, nod an assent, and after a moment Dan and I would look at each other and utter, "What'd he say?" We never could understand him in any way, shape or form. Even Izzy would chide him:

"Don't pay him no mind. He talks Geechee," Izzy would say, then burst out laughing and start to wheeze. Izzy was a heavy smoker. We were somewhat in awe of him not knowing the full extent of his "connections," but we sensed that he held a lot of sway. I also recall that at the time Charleston was a "dry" town, so the club was essentially a speakeasy. Beer and wine flowed freely, but hard spirits were on the taboo list.

We also were let in on a secret about Izzy. Being of overly ample girth, he became wedged in the bathtub one evening before coming to the club. His wife had tried in vain to get him out, and eventually had to call the fire department to free him. In her haste, she had failed to remove the armada of toy ducks and boats that were his playthings in the tub. The firemen got him free of the bondage, but they also spread the word about his childlike diversions. Once Dan and I heard about this, whenever Izzy would walk by, we'd make almost indistinguishable "quack" sounds, and snicker to ourselves.

While in Charleston we managed to meet other local musicians and vocalists. They would take us to an after-hour joint where both black and white musicians would jam. In the early 1950s, the south was still segregated, and one had to be careful where and how fraternization took place. I recall one female singer by the name of Sugar Holt who had come into the Carriage House to hear our group. Sugar was a fine singer with flaming red hair and an amazing resemblance to Rita Hayworth. Izzy introduced us and afterward she proceeded to ask Dan and I if we wanted to come to the late night jam. We agreed, and someone came by about midnight to take us to a back alley spot. This enabled us to meet and play with some of the locals, including bassist "Frenchy" Cauette. He had a full-sized upright bass with a hand carved lions head for a scroll. It sounded as big as a house, and having someone with a good instrument and good ears playing behind us was a novelty. We were accustomed to simply tuning out any sound below 200 cycles to preserve our sanity.

Charleston was a Navy town back then, and most of downtown was loaded with beer bars and bar girls "on the hustle." Some of them would spill over to the Carriage House, which by comparison, was an upscale supper club. As a neophyte with females, I was unaware of the complete picture, but I knew these girls were friendly. I found out just how "friendly" in due time. It was in Charleston at age eighteen that I had my first encounter into manhood. Others followed. In my frame of reference, Charleston was a huge success.

   Sabel & Dawson liked Dan and me, but wasn't too crazy about Tolly. We set up a deal for the following year, whereby Dan and I would return using "Frenchy" as our bassist. What we didn't know was that "Frenchy" had a drinking problem and over the course of an evening, he'd imbibe to the point of being unable to stand and play. He'd often fall asleep while standing, holding the massive lion's head bass to prop himself up. While all this was taking place, Dan and I did our best to keep the crowd entertained, even to the point of singing. Neither of us had a voice worthy of getting near a microphone, but we did so to keep from being just a pure jazz trio. My main thrust at that stage of life was dominated by hormones, and I became the proverbial Satyr, chasing everything that wore a skirt. I managed to get myself into some precarious situations in doing so, but Izzy's connections with law enforcement always managed to get me out of whatever trouble I had gotten into. One that comes to mind was mistaken identity. Bob Tolly decided to take a break from "Lady Macbeth" and have a fling with the checkroom girl at the Carriage House. A few days later while she was under the influence of a few too many beers, she blurted to her steady boyfriend that she'd had an affair with Bob from the band. He knew me, but had never met Tolly. Enraged, he came after me with a loaded gun. When word got out to Izzy, I had an escort, along with a couple of his "goons" at the hotel. One was stationed in the lobby and another on the roof. The enraged boyfriend was thwarted coming up the fire escape toward my room gun in hand. One of Izzy's handymen caught him and cooled him off by explaining that he had the wrong Bob. I didn't much care what happened after that. Now it was Tolly's problem.

   One downside of South Carolina was the proliferation of insects. Insects and I never developed an affinity. In fact, I hated them, especially ones that flew. Miller moths especially were annoying with their rapid circling and darting motions. One evening when Dan and I were in a local hash house having ordered chili at about one o'clock in the morning, a moth was busily circling a hanging light fixture above our table. My eyes kept following the damn thing as it came dangerously close to the hot bulb. The waitress finally arrived with our chili, and as I was about to sink my spoon into the bowl, the moth hit the bulb and proceeded to spiral downward, and looped smack into my chili, where it sank into the dark red goop. I thought Dan would wet his pants with laughter. I wasn't thrilled!

During a return trip to the Carriage House minus Bob Tolly, we were staying on the second floor of another old established hotel in Charleston. We had no refrigerator, so my brilliant solution to keep the beer cold was to suspend the cans in the toilet bowl and tie the flush handle upward, allowing a constant stream of cool water to wash over them. I proceeded to do so, and we went off to work. Upon returning four hours later, we found the lobby awash in water and a porter cleaning it up with a mop. Apparently one of the cans had slipped into the throat of the toilet bowl, plugging it enough so the water overflowed the bowl and cascaded into the lobby below. We were immediately ousted from those digs, and had to find another place to stay.

Our next haven was a relatively new high-rise, the Sergeant Jasper Apartments. It wasn't fancy, but we had a kitchen and it was decently furnished. I decided that we would save money by cooking in rather than eating three meals a day in restaurants. The thought of doing dishes and cleaning up was somewhat of a turnoff but I had a brilliant answer in theory: Buy paper plates and plastic utensils, and then simply chuck everything when the meal was over. A trip to the nearest market was next and supplies were purchased, along with breakfast food. Bacon & eggs. I could hardly wait!

The process of making breakfast was going smoothly until time came to turn the bacon. I did so with a plastic fork, which proceeded to melt into the bacon fat, rendering the whole serving useless. Another good idea shot to Hell! If anything good came from that experience it was my first exposure to food preparation, which in later years would become a happy diversion. Cooking was to become a hobby, something I still enjoy doing to this day.

When it came time to wrap up our engagement, we began packing our belongings at Sgt. Jasper's namesake building. Since we'd been partying quite a bit there were numerous bottles of various liquors with about one shot left in each bottle. Rather than pack these to take back to New York, I decided to finish them up. Understandably mixing rum, gin, vodka and rye in one sitting isn't a smart route to take and predictably, I became quite ill that evening. I awakened the following morning on my knees with my head dangling in the toilet bowl where apparently I'd spent the night. The pungent aftertaste of juniper berries from the gin was predominant and after the blue fumes cleared, I headed for a full pot of strong coffee, since Dan and I had to clear out that morning. On this trip I'd driven my old Chrysler to Charleston, and because Dan didn't have a drivers license, I knew I'd have to be the sole driver back to New York. I kept imagining that there was a blue haze on my windshield up until about the North Carolina border. I was relieved when I discovered it was a hangover, and eventually it disappeared.

During my maturing process I started to become more politically aware. The family I came from was staunch dyed-in-the-wool Republican, which in my earlier years meant absolutely nothing to me. All I knew about politics were the symbols, either an elephant or a donkey. I naturally assumed that since my grandparents were Republican, so was I. This began to change as I became savvier about the platforms that either embraced the working class or the big businessmen. Although a salaried employee, my grandfather felt that to be a Democrat was to identify with the immigrant population and the blue-collar workers. Since he was an employee of a brokerage in Manhattan, albeit as a clerk, he wanted to project an upper-class image so he would belittle anything democratic as being socialistic, or heaven forbid, Communist. After a lifetime of servitude to *Spencer Trask and Company*, he barely made sixty dollars a week at retirement time. There was no pension or profit sharing for him, only a meager social security check on which to live.

As a union member and having attended meetings with

other musicians, I slowly became aware of the fact that my basic middle-class strata was solely because of unionism and the benefits that pulled the worker-bees from slave labor to a respectable level of pay. In espousing my opinions at home, everyone from my mother on up decried my feelings as those of Communist influence and began to look toward my associates as the possible cause of my political blasphemy. Dan Fox as a resident of Greenwich Village was immediately suspect. My family never quite understood that liberalism is a phase that most young people go through at some point in their maturation process. They were sure that I was becoming a Communist. One has to take into account that this was the early '50s, the McCarthy era, when there was an alleged Communist conspiracy in every closet. The overall result of these divergent opinions was a further estrangement at home. In time, I would eventually become a "moderate," having conservative opinions on certain issues and more liberal ones on others. Meanwhile, my grandparents died in 1956 and 1957, having no worldly possessions except a $600 bank account, years of rent receipts and a 1939 Buick.

My fascination with the south hadn't ended, however. When I heard of an opening for a pianist with a hotel band heading down to Savannah, Georgia, I immediately applied. The leader was a nice chap named Lou Schroeder who tried to assemble a five-piece group to play a month at the original DeSoto Hilton, a Savannah landmark. At this time the city of Savannah was in a state of deterioration and the downtown restoration had yet to occur. Today the historic district is a beautiful sight to behold, but then it was largely some decrepit townhouses and ramshackle wooden structures that had been termite fodder for decades. The old DeSoto Hilton wasn't too far from that stage of rot either. A new sterile twelve-story edifice that doesn't seem to fit the surroundings has since replaced it. The old hotel was about five stories high and would have been perfect at a seaside location. The Sapphire Room was for dining and dancing, which was the location of our "Mickey Mouse" (society) band. There was a jazz scene happening in and around Savannah, but at the time I was not fortunate enough to meet anyone involved in that part of the music business.

Lou Schroder's band consisted of tenor sax, trumpet, violin, drums and piano. Having no bass player made it difficult for me to play anything decent and although I don't recall the generally mediocre personnel, I do recall the drummer. His name was Freddie, and he had been in World War I. His set of traps was also from that era and so was his playing. Freddie had been shell-shocked in the war, and traces of that would remain to spill over into this engagement. Occasionally in a spurt of musical enthusiasm, Freddie would give an unruffled *fortissimo* kick to the thirty-inch bass drum that had the painting of a girl in a hula skirt on the front. The resounding "boom" would put Freddie into a flashback of WWI. He'd drop his sticks, and fall to the floor holding his arms over his head. We'd have to then coax him up with assurances that the enemy had gone and he could continue playing. This was only one of many highly irregular musical personalities I would encounter through the years.

I wasn't too thrilled with Savannah in 1954 so when the time came to depart I did so gladly. I left the aging hotel and the over-the-hill tired group of hookers that used to frequent the hotel bar and made my way home to New York. Once back in Manhattan, I headed down to the union floor to see what else might be available. The contractor for bandleader Al Donahue approached me. Al Donahue had been a semi-name bandleader back in the 1930s and had since provided bands for cruise ships and hotels. "Did I want to go to Bermuda for six months?" he queried. The thought of Bermuda as some exotic place conjured up visions of beautiful babes and palm trees. The pay was $125 per week with room and board provided, so how bad could it be? I agreed to take it, but I was advised that if I failed to stay the entire six months, I would have to pay my own airfare round trip from New York. I didn't give this a second thought since I knew I'd be going to paradise! Besides, with no expenses I could save my money and perhaps buy that new car I had always wanted.

By now the blue and white Samsonite suitcase was getting a bit seedy, but it held together through the Lockheed Constellation's bumpy flight over the Atlantic. Upon landing in Bermuda I was met by sub-leader Tommy Norato, a violinist from New England who was in charge of the band at the Hotel St. George. I soon learned that St. George was at the uninhabited end of Bermuda, and the only guests were newlyweds and geriatrics. This was unwelcome news to a horny eighteen-year-old who had visions of a totally different scene.

The band was a quartet, once again minus a bassist. Violin, tenor sax, drums and piano comprised what later was to become known as "Tommy Norato and his Neurotics." The drummer who I was scheduled to share a room with was a nice, albeit simple Italian kid from the Bronx whose mother would mail him whole garlic-laden salamis. He stashed them under the bed, and in the wee hours would awaken and start chomping on a two-foot long giant sausage. His joy and delight was blowing realistic-sounding arm farts after the lights were turned off. At first I thought they were real, thinking the salami was creating an adverse gastric reaction. I would think to myself, "What the Hell was that?" I found out it was his own little joke that wore out before long.

The saxophonist was a capable player who was a plumber by trade in Cleveland, Ohio. What he was doing there was never totally ascertained but there he was, night after night. His personality was that of misfit, a kind of *nebbish* that went along with the other members of the band. It made me start wondering about myself. Was I some sort of neurotic reject from society? If I hadn't been when I accepted the Bermuda engagement, I felt sure I would be at the end of the six-month commitment.

We played for dinner and then dancing afterward. Norato had a hearing problem, both aurally and musically. He was too proud to wear a hearing aid so we had to repeat everything we said at least once. On many a tune he'd slide well past the destined pitch on his violin and I'd cringe. He'd say,

"What are you complaining about? I'm closer to it than you are!"

If there was one thing in his favor, he had a decent sense of humor.

The St. George Hotel had very little going for it. Passing the time was difficult since there was no television, and only two government run radio stations. The staff looked upon the band disdainfully since we were earning at least three times the average Bermudan's salary. The wait staff and the chef resented the fact that we would eat from the menu three times daily, so if there was a piece of meat that had turned rancid you could be certain it would get served to us. My salvation was the local liquor store. After I found out that they would fill a Pepsi-cola bottle with black rum right out of the cask for fifty cents, I'd make a daily trip down the hill right after lunch. This would keep me high enough to get by the day, while I'd lounge around the lobby wishing I'd never accepted the job. I endured a hurricane, gigantic yellow spiders, tarantulas and every other sort of flying critter that inhabited the island. Giant cockroaches abounded and rats scurried up and down in the ivy fighting the cockroaches for dinner. Around Easter, the cockroaches (or water bugs as the Chamber of Commerce refers to them) sprouted wings and flew about in search of mates. If they had any vision at all, it couldn't have been very good, since they'd fly slowly, come directly at one and never veer away. I can't begin to tell you how many of them managed to fly into me, and I became increasingly jumpy. I later learned that the last pianist had wandered off one day and was never heard from again. I began to see how that could occur, as I was about ready for a screened-in rest home.

On Wednesdays we had to traipse over to the Castle Harbour Hotel, where we gained a fifth member, a bassist. This helped a bit musically, but as fate would have it a third cousin on my mother's side, Howard Hohl, was the manager of the Castle Harbour. Howard was a hotelier who never seemed to hold a job for any period of time. As I got to know him I understood the reason why. He was likeable yet ineffective, a prime example of

The Peter Principle: Keep getting promoted until you reach your own level of incompetence, and there you stay! Howard was no help at all in solving any problem, and his out for every situation was to pull a police whistle from his pocket, blow it and yell, "Everyone in the pool!" He'd then laugh and walk on to the next item on his agenda.

This proved to be the longest six months I'd ever have to endure and when the term of my contract was complete, the T.W.A. Constellation on the runway looked like a shining star, one that was to carry me back to civilization and normal sized Brooklyn cockroaches.

CHAPTER 6

GREENWICH VILLAGE ADVENTURES

Back in the mid 1950s Greenwich Village was a hotbed of entertainment. Situated in the lower part of Manhattan, every type of nightclub lined the main arteries that wove through this eclectic neighborhood. Jazz clubs, strip-tease joints, folk singing hangouts for the college crowd, and even one place on West 8th Street dubbed "The Village Barn." The wage scale provided by the union was somewhat lower in all the venues within Greenwich Village and to this day, I'll never understand why. I think some of the well-connected club owners paid off the right people. To play six hours a night, six nights per week paid $76.50. Meanwhile the clubs uptown were paying about $125.00 for similar conditions. The only advantage to the situation was that younger musicians just starting out would get hired because the established players wouldn't think of working for such low wages.

New York City mandated that anyone working in a cabaret, nightclub or any establishment serving liquor must be in possession of what was known as a Cabaret Card. Anyone who has ever ridden in a New York taxi surely has noticed the 3x5 hack license, which always contained a mug shot of the driver. The people taking those photos at the license bureau were proud that they made everyone look like an ex-felon. Pat Boone would have looked like axe murderer had he applied for a hack license. The cabaret licenses were issued in the same building, same office, by the same photographer. The only difference was that instead of mounting it on a dashboard, we had to keep it in a wallet. The underworld was notorious for owning and running nightclubs and for reasons unknown, these cards were supposed to keep "undesirables" from getting a foothold in the nightclub scene. About all it really did was keep musicians who may have been caught smoking marijuana at one time from earning a reasonable living. The mob still ran the clubs. I plodded through the forms, got fingerprinted, photographed and finally got my card. I could now pass for Dillinger.

The first job offer I had came from Hal Graham, a bandleader who held forth at The Village Barn. This was a cavernous place about two stories high, which was actually the basement and first floor combined. It was cleverly decorated to resemble an urban architect's vision of an actual barn, and busloads of tourists would flock to it nightly. I can recall having been taken there to celebrate my 10th birthday by members of my family. It was built to entertain the masses, and the masses were often delivered by the busload.

Aside from Hal Graham's dance band which was a five-piece ensemble consisting of piano, bass, drums, tenor sax and multi-instrumentalist Graham (trumpet, vibes, piano and mellophone) the big draw was square dancing with a caller named Piute Pete. During our intermission a small group of quasi-hillbillies would take the bandstand and play the usual do-si-do repertoire while Pete got the tourists on the floor for square dancing plus other fun and games. During these breaks the other band members and I would go outside on West 8th Street and gawk at the array of tourists, gays and panhandlers that made up most of the foot traffic. The Village was the center of New York's non-conformist society, and there were always strange sights to behold.

Our saxophonist Marty Holmes was a fine jazz player who subjugated his real talents to earn a living. Working with Hal Graham was a strange experience; Hal played a multitude of instruments, none of them well. He fancied himself a jazz player on the mellophone but in actuality, whenever he picked it up and started to play the sound resembled an irate elephant more than jazz. His piano playing (we would do twin pianos) was usually laced with wrong chords and it was not exactly a joy for me to accompany him. Attached to the piano allocated to me was a unique device called an Organo. It sounded similar to a Hammond organ but was connected to the piano and controlled by a paddle under the keyboard that I operated with my knee. One downside to this job was that I was constantly wearing a hole in the right knee of my blue suit from having it rub on the underside of the piano while using the Organo. We would actually, believe it or not, do radio broadcasts three times weekly from this location. All this for a whopping $76.50 per week!

The drummer was a good-looking Italian chap named Lou Fiorella. He sang in a pleasant baritone voice, and was easy to get to know. He was also what in Italian is called a *stunade,* a term given to someone who's mentally about one beat off. The word translates to "stunned," and usually refers to somebody who's been whacked on the head with a two-by-four and hasn't fully recovered. You'd tell Lou a joke and get very little reaction, if any. About five minutes later he'd break out in a roar of laughter; it took the gag that long to permeate his senses. He came from a first generation immigrant family from the Bronx and lived on the fourth floor of a tenement with his mother. She spoke no English and commuted daily to a garment sweatshop. His one brother Sal was in the slammer, having made his living as a "wise guy" for the local mafia. The younger brother Pete was a bright fellow, probably destined for a role in the brainier end of the aforementioned organization, possibly as an accountant. Lou and I struck up a friendship that would extend well over the ensuing years, with the both of us working in the Catskill Mountains together as well as many years of playing nightclubs. It lasted until his untimely demise at age 49 from lung cancer.

The Horowitz brothers, Meyer and Larry, owned the Village Barn. The waiters wore red and white striped shirts with elastic armbands, and a nightly ritual before the place opened was for them to line up and walk past Meyer with one arm raised high. Meyer would in turn take a whiff from each waiter's armpit to make sure they had no body odor that might offend a potential customer. Larry was a bit more demure, always well tuxedoed and seemingly very much in control. The only thing that wasn't under control was a rooster whose cage sat up near the spotlight in the back of the club. One impressionist-comic, Dick Capri always complained that as he'd reach a punch line the rooster would crow loudly, diverting the audience from appreciating his joke and instead, laughing at the rooster. He was always threatening to come in early and put it in the soup pot.

The emcee was Larry McMahon, a middle-aged Irishman who had the geniality of an Arthur Godfrey. He tried a bit of humor but he had bad delivery and it never quite got off the ground. His job was to make the crowd feel comfortable which he did, and to introduce the array of dancers, singers and comics who were a part of the floor show. I put in a year working at the Barn before I had my fill of Graham & Co.

My next offer came from *Tony Pastors'*, a club on West 3rd Street that was in transition from jazz to striptease. The joint was owned by a "well-connected" guy named Joe Cataldo, a.k.a. "Joe the Wop." Joe reputedly ran the numbers racket in the New York area, and had his hand in a number of clubs in both the village and uptown on 52nd Street. I took Lou Fiorella with me to Pastors from the Village Barn, and enlisted the services of a blonde female bassist who also sang. The term "bassist" is not exactly what she should have been called; She owned a bass that was painted white, and to the best of my recall it had never been tuned. If it had, it wouldn't have sounded any different since she apparently learned the bass from whoever taught Bob Tolly. In other words, she didn't know one note from another but she'd snap the strings in time with what the rest of us were doing, and with her low-cut gowns she could visually please an audience of non-music aficionados who weren't listening for accurate bass notes. We had publicity photos taken, and called ourselves

"The Encores." Musically this individual would not be my first choice, but sex and singing always outsold pure jazz.

The ENCORES

We'd play an hour set, and then we'd take an hour off. That's when the other trio would begin their stint backing the strippers. This went on nicely for a couple of months. One evening as we played a newly learned ballad called "Invitation," word came from one of the bouncers that the boss liked that tune. "Play it every set, *capiche?*" I certainly did. Cataldo, although not a big man in stature had a gaze that could penetrate a steel girder. I didn't choose to be the recipient of that laser beam. We played "Invitation" religiously every set. During the time we'd be doing our best at playing jazz the strippers would circulate among the male habitués soliciting drinks. The male patrons would purchase a split of champagne for the stripper with whom he'd be seated next to, and she would surreptitiously proceed to spill most of it between the cushions of the booth while simultaneously diverting his attention. The other drink of choice was brandy and Coke. Both liquids were approximately the same color, and that allowed the "spit-back" technique. The girl would take a sip of the brandy and proceed to assumedly use the Coke as a chaser. In reality the mouthful of brandy would end up being spit back into the Coke glass, which is why these women could seemingly drink all night and never appear inebriated. Meanwhile, the "johns" would be getting more stoned as their drinks kept arriving at the table. They were actually drinking them. If a patron was a good enough tipper, he'd be escorted to a dark table in a corner of the club and experience some sexual manipulation while a long tablecloth covered the action. The small bottles of cheap champagne would go on the tab for $25.00 apiece, which provided a big surprise for the gentleman buyer at the end of the evening. Usually the girl would seemingly consume three or four while sitting with the same sucker.

Our blonde so-called bassist was not always there, and often I'd have to call last minute subs. My regular sub was Tom O'Neill, who really knew the instrument and played well. I'd look forward to when our gal had her snits and would decide not to come in, so I could feel a musical foundation and hear correct notes emanating from the instrument. One night Tom was unavailable so he decided to send in a young bassist who had recently arrived in New York upon discharge from the Navy. This substitute arrived with his bass cover in tatters and the bass held together with strapping tape. In a "hoosier" dialect right out of Indiana, he greeted me with,

"Howdy! You Bob Alberti?"

"Howdy" sounded more like "Heidy." Hearing that sound, checking out the oversized electric-blue suit on this underweight refugee from the Midwest, my first thought was "What in Hell did Tom send me now?" He peeled off what remained of the rag-tag bass cover, tuned up and began to join me on the first number. I can't tell in words how overjoyed I was. This fellow had great ears, good time, and sensed just about every place I'd choose to go musically. I'd land on it, he'd be there. This led me to a very easy decision. Blondie was about to become history. This was the new third member of the trio. He didn't look as if he'd be able to wear low-cut dresses so I had the bouncer pull the publicity photo from the front window of Tony Pastor's bistro and decided instead to concentrate more on the jazz aspect rather than the entertaining trio. This chap's name is Al Hood, and through the years he has remained one of my closest friends.

Directly across 3rd Street was another club, 'The Heat Wave' that was also owned by Cataldo. Occasionally a musical crisis would arise when a pianist didn't show up, or one who couldn't read the strippers' music would have been sent in as a substitute. I'd get the "order" from our maitre' de at Tony Pastors' that as soon as our set had finished, I was to run across and play the 'Heat Wave' show. Knowing the powers that be, I would acquiesce with a smile. I wasn't the greatest reader but by this time I'd become show-wise and could pretty well fake my way through whatever was required. This type of night meant six solid hours of work with a stop at the restroom if I was lucky. The leader at 'The Heat Wave' (later to become the renowned "Blue Note" jazz club) was saxophonist Jack Dema. We struck up a friendship that's still in flourishing almost fifty years later.

One piece of luck that I inherited was an audiographic memory for music. All I had to do was hear a song a few times on the radio, and it was locked in to my musical memory bank forever. By the time I was in my early twenties, I probably knew a thousand songs and could play them in any key. This came to the attention of Jack Dema who had been busy in New York's club date industry. A club date was a name given to any single engagement at a hotel or catering hall, usually a wedding, Bar Mitzvah, anniversary party or a convention. Bands would be assembled for the likes of society leaders Lester Lanin, Meyer Davis, Mark Towers, Stanley Melba, Steven Scott, etc. They paid considerably better than the night clubs, and I found that the wage scale was over a hundred dollars for one night's work in this field. This was an attractive alternative to the Village wage scale that by now had gone up to $87.50 for a thirty-six hour workweek.

Jack Dema had worked out a deal at The Heat Wave whereby he would take off to do a club date, paying a small stipend to the sax player in the alternating band to cover for him until he arrived later in the evening when his club date finished. He approached me with an offer that would be similar. He'd introduce me to the club date leaders and I could work out a schedule with the pianist in the other band to cover for me until I finished my club date. Financially, this sounded like a great way to finally get ahead of the creditors, so I left Tony Pastor's and headed to The Heat Wave. This meant a change in direction from the world of jazz that I so dearly loved, but I also liked to eat well, and the world of commercial music could provide a chance to live a better life. I decided it was worth a try. This particular establishment was the one that I referred to when the anonymous phone call from Chicago interrupted my sleep with the warning to keep my hands off the hatcheck girl!

At this stage in my life, I was probably going through the most difficult time personally and psychologically. The youthful expectations and dreams had given way to the anger and realization that the world out there wasn't what I'd expected. The acne was hanging on even into my early twenties and the baby-fat hadn't disappeared as I hoped it would. I was searching and coming up empty for some positive path for my life to follow. It was about this time that I began to read about psychology and psychotherapists. On a friend's recommendation, I began to see a therapist in Brooklyn, which turned out to be the beginning of a lengthy quest for insight into the recesses of my mind. Why was I always choosing females who were more messed up than I was? I had a hard enough time keeping myself somewhat above water, and it seemed that whomever I chose to date looked at me as a cure-all for their hang-ups. I would then proceed to crumble emotionally with the combined weight of my problems and those that the girl-of-the-month would lay on my lap. Much was due, I suppose, to the maladjusted household in which I was raised, and I guess there were some unexplored dark corners to work through.

Part of the therapy evolved into a period of estrangement from my family. I had to break down the old patterns before I could establish new ones. It was as if I had to come clean with my feelings, no matter how the family would have reacted. As could be expected, they didn't react well and I cut off communications with all my relatives. The unfortunate side was this also extended to my Uncle Bob, as I had to re-examine my relationship with him. I received most of my attention from him when I was a child and felt very close to him, perhaps more so than to any other member of my family. His marriage when I was about eleven years old, along with his move to Nassau County in Long Island created a long physical distance. They had a daughter Phyllis, and naturally his propensity for nurturing turned to her. He had also begun to imbibe rather heavily so that when we would meet, he'd have a vague stare that stifled our lines of communication. His wife had become a tippler, and to add to the alcoholic mix his mother-in-law had also moved in with them. The mother-in-law was an all-time evil drunkard, making my decision not to visit them quite easy. Family gatherings became one big drunken hate-spewing brawl, and I finally severed all contact and broke away from the immediate family. Whenever my mother would add her presence to the drunken family gathering, sparks would fly, as she was always extremely jealous of Uncle Bob's college education and his success in business. She would be the catalyst to an all-out family war. Alcohol seemed to have a way of releasing venom from most of my family members.

From that point forward, I would build relationships on

level ground, no longer having to start off as the underdog within the family. I reached a level in my development where I called my own shots, not my mother. My involvement with therapy and self-improvement was an ongoing process that would last into succeeding years. It was a turning point that took me from self-loathing to self-assuredness, and allowed my future career to be more successful. This type of emotional adjustment didn't come overnight. Sometimes it was necessary to see someone for periodic tune-ups before it totally sunk in and became second nature. I'm grateful to therapist Dr. Milton Shapiro for the tremendous help and understanding along the way.

CHAPTER 7

THE CLUB-DATE BIZ

The union floor seemed huge. By night it was the Roseland Ballroom. On Mondays, Wednesdays and Fridays the afternoons were given over to Local 802 of the Musicians Union, who had leased offices on the second floor. Between twelve noon and three o'clock in the afternoon, musicians from the surrounding boroughs and counties would arrive and walk to various areas in the ballroom. The union floor had sectors defined by the type of work one did. Technically it was called the exchange floor. Musicians seeking employment would gather to meet with the individual contractors and hopefully find gigs.

As you walked in the main entry, the big-band section loomed immediately in front. Just past that was the Latino section, the freelancers who played the Palladium in Manhattan, Soldier Myers in Brooklyn and other dance halls featuring bands such as Tito Puente, Tito Rodriguez, Machito and Noro Morales. Turning to the right you would find the contractors and musicians who regularly worked the catering halls or wedding factories in the Bronx, Brooklyn and Queens. These were primarily Jewish functions, and the musicians had to be well versed in the music of the Eastern European traditions: Horas, frailachs, sherrs and the traditional *shtick* that was all a part of a Jewish wedding or Bar Mitzvah. In the New York music scene, the definition of a *club-date* is any single engagement done for a private party or an organization. This includes debutante parties, dances, weddings, bar mitzvahs, political rallies, fund-raisers and a host of other types of occasions.

Going a few yards further toward the far end of the hall, one encountered the society leaders. These were the high-paying club-date offices that had a lock on the debutante balls and house parties in the Hamptons on Long Island where the Fortune "400" had summer estates and Park Avenue connections. Leaders such as Ben Cutler, Meyer Davis, Lester Lanin and Stanley Melba managed to capture probably about eighty percent of the functions given by graduates of prep schools and Ivy League colleges. Each leader would have as many as ten bands out playing parties in any given evening, all using the name of the well known leader. Despite the fact that most of the clientele were WASPs, all the leaders were Jewish. The story goes that one dowager who was interviewing Lester Lanin asked,

"Mr. Lanin, are you Jewish?"

To which Lester unhesitatingly replied, "Not necessarily!"

The society bands had one basic tempo, and would play continuous music for five and six hours a night. The scale for a *continuous* as it was called was considerably higher than a job that had intermissions. It allowed only a five-minute respite out of the hour and these breaks could be added up and taken cumulatively. Every musician had to know another instrument (preferably one of the rhythm section,) so in case there was a bathroom break needed, someone else would take over that instrument while the primary player attended to nature's call.

All songs had to fit into that bounce tempo, regardless of how ill suited they may have been to that pace. "September Song," a poignant ballad was played in the same tempo as "Just In Time." "Tenderly" was in a medley with "Get Me to the Church On Time," played as though it was on a turntable at the wrong speed. Musicality was out the window. The focus was to get those dancers in their waistcoats on the dance floor, and keep the party going at that tempo. That was paramount in the eyes of the leaders.

The most amazing part of the club-date industry was

when they put together large ensembles. There was no music to read. Each player had to know the entire repertoire of club date music. There were instrumental specialists who would diligently learn the harmony part to every song that might be called to play. One must imagine the vast amount of music a player had to memorize. The required repertoire encompassed just about every show tune of the 20th century, and each player had to know the specific harmony part to which they were assigned. For instance some players were specialized "third-alto" players. They had to reel off the third alto sax part by memory for whatever tunes the leader called. The same went for the brass players. Second trumpet, third trombone all had the discipline and the talent to pull off such a laborious feat. Sometimes this would lead to an unintentional disaster. At one party a patron requested a song that most of the band didn't know. The only musician who knew the song was the third alto player. He proudly strode up to the microphone and proceeded to play the third alto harmony part, which bore little if any resemblance to the actual melody of the song itself. As it turned out the patron who made the request didn't know the difference. So went some of the more humorous events that can happen on any given club date. It was far from an artistic wonder, rather like watching a dog walk on its hind legs. You know it's not going to be done well, but you're amazed that it gets done at all.

Another mandatory portion of playing a club-date was called *strolling* and every pianist had to double on accordion. When the various courses of food were served, the dance music would stop. The strollers immediately went into their alternative mode as the pianist hoisted up the squeeze-box, (a.k.a. accordion) the bassist moved out onto the dining area, and usually one violinist would join as the trio would walk from table to table playing a host of Hungarian Gypsy selections. This would continue until the diners had finished the particular course, at which point we'd scurry back to the bandstand and resume dance medleys in the same tempo we had recently ended.

I had a reputation of being the second worst accordion player in New York. The worst was rumored to be Moe Wechsler, and I assume it was because he probably hated the instrument as much as I did. I would leave my accordion in the trunk of my car, which resulted in the reeds freezing in the wintertime. When I would first take it out and start to play, there were no notes coming out, only a loud asthmatic wheeze. The leaders would glare at me in horror and disgust, and I'd simply shrug and say,

"It has a cold!"

Years later when I decided to move to California, I orchestrated a ceremony to be remembered: Leaving New York by car, I pulled over along the East River Drive and heaved the accordion, case and all into the river with a solemn vow; I would never again play an accordion. I never have, and I often wonder if it became a home for wayward, wheezing fish.

Of all the club-date leaders, the one who was least liked by most musicians was Lester Lanin. One of seven brothers, he was a miserly weasel with little regard for his musicians. The brothers were estranged from one another at the urging of their mother, a rather paranoid woman who set the brothers against one another, perhaps to hone their predatory business acumen. Some of the other brothers also entered the music business. Willie became a piano tuner with a stuttering speech defect and two others, Howard and Jimmy became club date leaders in Washington D.C. and Philadelphia, respectively. I had to audition for Lester before being considered eligible for employment with any of his bands. In his office was an old out-of-tune upright piano, on which I had to pound out some show tunes for his approval. The *piece-de-resistance* of a Lanin audition was having to play an obscure song titled *Dirty Lady*. If you could play that, you were part of the organization. Fortunately, I was forewarned about this quirk of his, and I had the song down pat.

Lester Lanin had a virtual lock on society events for many decades and would send out numerous bands in one evening, all with the same repertoire of dance music. He had his "first" band, consisting of talented but mischievous players who were his primary musicians. The other bands he'd put together could all play the same type of music but were under the sub-leadership of his various henchmen. I was not part of the basic group but was, on many occasions, part of one of the satellite groups he'd send out under the Lester Lanin name.

Lester abhorred drinking, and always instructed the bartenders not to serve anything to the musicians except club soda and ginger ale. Knowing this, we'd collect a few dollars and slip it to the bartender, who would substitute scotch and vodka in water tumblers. We'd sip those throughout the night, with Lester never understanding how we could get so whacko on soft drinks.

One of the drummers was Irv Goldberg, a little fellow with a cleft palate, making his speech a bit hard to understand. Lester would constantly pick on him for one thing or another knowing that he couldn't yell back, or if he did, nobody would understand what he said. One night, in the middle of a set, Lanin looked up to see Goldberg with a big sign around his neck, that read:

"PLEASE DO NOT DISTURB THE ANIMALS!"

Among the more colorful characters was Russell "Big Chief" Moore, a full-blooded Indian who played trombone. Moore had a fondness for cigarettes and although smoking was *verboten* on the bandstand, he'd manage to light up whenever possible, usually when Lester was busy schmoozing with one of the society matrons. During a Lanin date at the Waldorf-Astoria Hotel, the Catholic Church had lost a leader and the Cardinals were in conclave. Once again, Moore lit up a cigarette and a huge puff of white smoke emerged from the brass section. At this moment, Lester glanced up, and yelled,

"What's going on back there?"

From the depths of the rear stage riser, Moore yelled back,

"We're electing a pope!"

Probably the greatest protagonist at tormenting Lanin was John Plonsky, a fine trumpet player who subsequently moved to California and became a studio composer (John Parker.) He had a sharp mind and a warped sense of humor, and his greatest delight was to cause misery for Lanin. For example, at Lanin's modest office on West 57th street, he had a secretary who was fairly promiscuous. The lady apparently had transmitted a case of gonorrhea to one of the band musicians, which the unfortunate chap treated as soon as he could. Shortly thereafter, Plonsky found out about it and approached her, not as a reprimand but to do him a favor; He'd taken up a collection from the band members to give to her if she'd sleep with Lanin before having it cured. Despite the generous offer she refused, referring to Lanin as "that little creep" and proceeded to pass on the monetary reward.

One of Plonsky's subtle schemes involved creating a signal with the rest of the band, whereby the brass section would modulate a half tone higher every four measures, while simultaneously the saxes would drop down a half tone. This usually occurred when Lanin was busy chatting with a society matron, having shifted his attention away from the music. Lanin didn't have the greatest ears in the music business, having been a half-baked drummer in his playing days. The band would continue this tonality spread every four bars until Lanin innately thought something sounded wrong. As soon as he would snap his head around with a quizzical look toward the musicians, almost as one they would resolve back into the normal key, as if nothing unusual had occurred.

Since much of Lanin's evening was taken up with socializing at the corner of the bandstand, he would still make an effort to call the tunes out to the band, so they'd know what to play next. If he didn't, the rhythm section would simply vamp ad nauseam until the next song was called. Plonsky would hear the next song, and rather than start from the beginning of the tune, he'd play only the last eight measures. The long vamp of relative nothingness would begin. Lanin would hear this happening behind him, knowing that he'd called out a song, and subconsciously he'd heard the end of it. He couldn't figure out why it went by so rapidly, and he'd say,

"I just called 'Just One of Those Things'!"

Plonsky would reply, "We just played it, Lester!"

Having heard the last eight bars, Lanin began doubting his own sanity.

Lester Lanin had a penchant for overcoats with fur neckpieces and homburg hats. They often would disappear by the end of an evening, bewildering Lester. I know of one occasion where the answer was evident, and it was when Plonsky "accidentally" sailed a hat onto the sidewalk from the Starlight Roof of the Waldorf Astoria where the band happened to be playing one winter night.

Another of his regulars was Jerry Pachtor, a talented saxophonist who doubled as a violinist. Jerry was also a "certified detractor" of Lester, and would do anything he possibly could to make sure Lester never had a moment's peace. During one engagement at the St. Regis Roof in the classy Manhattan Hotel of the same name, Jerry managed to get some eggs deposited in Lester's homburg. He apparently thought the best way to dispose of the evidence was to fling the hat (and a fur-collared overcoat) to the street below where some homeless indigent probably though this was *manna from heaven*. The following evening as the band assembled for another job, Lester, who had walked home the previous evening (as he usually did rather than take a cab) announced, "I'm turning this over to the F.B.I.!" The perpetrators feigned coughing fits to stifle their hysterical laughs.

Although Lanin was by all estimates a multi-millionaire, the years that I knew him he resided in a one-room apartment in a walk-up building on the upper east side of Manhattan. He had nails in the wall that served as a place to hang up his tuxedos. After I'd moved to California in 1959, I had heard that he made his first attempt at marriage to a lady who as I recall, was from Texas, and had very expensive tastes. Much to Lester's chagrin she proceeded to set up a luxurious lifestyle for the two of them. They later divorced, and you can guess who got the deluxe co-op.

The tales from the Lanin snake pit are rivaled only by the

stories from the Lawrence Welk band. Jokingly, rumor has it
that Welk was "the first semiconductor." Not far from the
truth! Never having worked with the Welk outfit, I only heard
the tales from a group of my California buddies who had spent
time with the Welk organization. That's a whole other story.
The big, happy family was in actuality a "Peyton Place!" Welk's
misreading of cue cards and unintentional off-color phrases are
legendary. His show was live (as opposed to taped) and whatever
went out over the air couldn't be changed.

A typical faux pas was his reading of a cue card from a
nostalgic show that featured music from World War I.

As Lawrence spoke it, the words were,

"Here's a lovely medley of songs from World War Eye!"

At another time, trombonist Barney Liddell was in front
of the band playing a lengthy solo. The stage manager signaled
Lawrence that they were running late, and to cut the number
short. Lawrence walked up to Barney from behind, took him by
the elbow and said in his inimitable dialect,

"I'm sorry, but we're running late, so I'm going to have to
jerk you off."

Too late! That had already hit every living room in suburban
America.

There are myriads of tales of a similar fashion that have
become folklore among the musicians in Hollywood who for so
many years worked on the Lawrence Welk show. I'd heard that
one summer when they did a tour of one-nighters traveling by
charter bus, they carried a staff psychiatrist along for the entire
tour. There was everything from wife swapping to one member
who had a penchant for pre-pubescent boys. Lawrence kept
espousing that they were "One big, happy family." I suppose
this was either the ultimate denial or sheer obliviousness. I can't
say that Lawrence was a great musician, nor was he respected
within the industry, but he somehow had his finger on the
pulse of commercialism, and managed to transform the Welk
organization into a national treasure for the geriatric set.

Throughout the four years that I spent doing club dates
I also kept a spot open with Jack Dema at The Heat Wave, so

whenever I didn't have anything that paid better, I'd go in to Greenwich Village and knock off a shift for the strippers. By now the schedule had been altered. Since the club's hours were 9 PM to 4 AM, rather than alternating hour-on/hour-off shifts, each trio was set to play continuously for three-and-a-half hours. The early shift was nine to twelve-thirty, with the next band picking up from twelve-thirty to four in the morning. I usually opted for the late shift, since most club dates were finished by midnight and I could usually get there in time to start. If I had a later club date, I worked it out with the first shift pianist to stay on and cover the piano chair until I got there. This worked out for a good period of time, until a singer who was dating the boss took a liking to my piano accompaniment. When I wasn't there to play for her, she'd whine and whimper to Joe Cataldo, which would clue him in that I wasn't there as often as I should be. On certain busy weeks, I may have showed up one or two nights out of six. This didn't sit too well with Cataldo, who sent word to Jack Dema that if I was going to keep this up, he'd have to get rid of me. Jack, being a loyal friend, refused to hand me that ultimatum and subsequently, Cataldo fired the trio, Jack included. I've never forgotten the loyalty shown by Jack at that time. I still regard him as a good pal and I visit him in Florida every chance I get.

The dismissal was somewhat of a shock, since the club had been my security blanket, especially if the club date season was lean. The summer was one of those seasons where virtually nothing happened with private partics, which was why we all would take summer resort jobs, either in the mountains or by the seashore.

After having spent seven years in the Catskills, I was offered a seashore job at a hotel in Spring Lake, New Jersey with club date leader Sonny Kippe. I was ready for a change, as I'd just about worn out my fascination with the Catskills. With hormones still raging, I was constantly disappointed with my success ratio in the Catskills resorts. Most of the young ladies who would vacation there were hoping to find a young man with some noble profession in his future. The job of a musician didn't seem to fit the image, so I had many a barren summer.

We had a happy little group at the Allaire Hotel by the seashore in Spring Lake, New Jersey. My good buddy Al Hood was hired on bass, and along with Eddie Pistilli on tenor and Don Beam on drums, and despite my feelings about accordions, Sonny's accordion couldn't daunt my enthusiasm to keep the music swinging. We stayed at an ancient Victorian rooming house run by Alice & Howard, a couple who owned this eighteenth century former Pony Express stop. The floors sloped, the bathroom was shared and the kitchen was communal. Nonetheless, the camaraderie was evident, and the summer passed fleetingly. It was in Spring Lake that I met Frances, who was eventually to become my first wife.

My first big mistake.

CHAPTER 8

LIFE'S REAL LESSONS

Being a young adult has one advantage; you don't truly know how dumb and inexperienced you are. It doesn't take long to come to some nasty truths, especially when trying to neatly fit into society.

When I was in my early twenties most of my friends had gotten married and were riding the subway to work each day with lunch bucket in tow. Returning home in the evening they'd stop off at O'Sullivan's Bar and Grill in Bay Ridge, have a couple of beers, and go home to whatever scene they had created in their respective marriages. While they had been legitimizing themselves, I'd been floating around from one neurotic lady to another. Greenwich Village had a plethora of non-conformists who were into the hip art scene while living in unheated walk-up hovels. Somehow they found me or I found them. I was out of one scene and into another, frustratingly unsatisfactory to all parties concerned. At the time I was occupying a lovely one-bedroom apartment in Flagg Court, a large high rise with an outdoor pool in the center courtyard. For Brooklyn this was quite an unusual setup, as the lifestyle generally didn't lend itself to outdoor sunbathing.

My bassist friend Al Hood had just gone through a dissolution with his first wife, who had relinquished the marriage vows and duties of motherhood to go to Italy and continue her quest to be an operatic diva. Al had sent his daughter Vicki who was about four at the time to live with his parents in Indiana, and as a result was somewhat at loose ends. Hearing this, I told him that he was welcome to bunk in at my place until he decided what he wanted to do. He did so, sleeping on the couch while his bass was propped up in a corner of the bedroom. He unwittingly chose the corner nearest the radiator to rest the bass, which gradually dried out the glue that held it together. One night while I was sound asleep there was a resounding explosion that startled the hell out of me. I looked around the room, and the bass was in pieces, scattered about. I ran into the living room, shouting to Al,

"Hey, man...Wake up! Your bass just blew up!"

He surveyed the damage, and despite the tragedy, I broke into howls of laughter. The thought of an exploding bass conjures up some potentially funny scenes, and somehow I just lost control at the absurdity of the situation. It wasn't quite as humorous to Al since this was the instrument with which he earned his living. I imagine his thoughts were about the cost of having the bass reconstructed and the length of time he'd be without the instrument. After surveying the damage, we each took a hit from the scotch bottle, and settled back to zonk out for the rest of the night. At least it would no longer be held together with duct tape.

Since I'd spurned the Catskills and opted for a summer gig at the Allaire Hotel in Spring Lake, New Jersey, I'd hoped to have more success dating young ladies. It was only about two hours from New York City and provided a different environment. The working guys and gals would take a commuter train as they got off work on Fridays, and lined up at the bar as the band played songs of the day by the postage-stamp dance floor. Dominico Modugno's version of *"Volare"* was the hit that summer. It was there in Spring Lake, New Jersey playing at The Allaire Hotel in the summer of 1957, I met Frances, the woman who was to become my first wife. I don't know if I was ever really in love with her, nor do I have the slightest recall of the wedding day. She was four years my senior, and I think the pangs of potential spinsterhood had descended on her. We dated for about six months, never consummating anything other than a bit of harmless but frustrating necking. I honored her request to remain chaste until after marriage, which I later regretted.

As I look back on our relationship, I recall that Frances was never at ease at any given time. I guess the term "up tight" would best describe her controlled demeanor when we were together. Unfortunately, I was just twenty-one and too inexperienced to react with concern to outward negative signs that were all too apparent at the time. Other friends and associates hinted at her manner of behavior in a questioning way, but I brushed off any possibilities that this may not have been my most prudent choice. Even Sonny Kippe tried warning me in a very diplomatic way that I might be making a big mistake, but I didn't want to hear it.

After we had wed, aside from her total non-passionate responses, she soon decided that something was wrong. I agreed but we weren't talking about the same problems. She complained that all her friends went out and partied on Friday and Saturday nights. We didn't. I didn't fit into the "Joe Lunchpail" mold. She had a solution: I should attend barber college and go into business with her father who owned the local barbershop in the Long Island community where she lived.

"Umm, excuse me," I said. "What was I doing when you and I met?"

"Playing in a band," she answered.

"Do you recall what night it was?"

"Either Friday or Saturday. I know my girlfriends and I were there for the weekend."

"That's what I do! I'm a musician! I make my living on weekend nights. If you wanted a barber for a husband, you should have married one. You don't marry a musician and ask him to change a career so you can go out on weekends."

The situation seemed pretty clear at this point. She was not going to adapt well to being a musician's wife. The fantasy of glamour that some people attach to those of us in show business can fade rapidly as the reality sets in. In addition she had never really broken the emotional and physical tie to her widowed father. She had a driving need to be his housekeeper and caretaker, neither of which he really required. He was able-bodied and had another daughter living at home who was a far better housekeeper than Frances. She'd finish her work as a legal secretary and go directly to her father's house, cook dinner for him, then come home to me. By that time she was too tired to make dinner for me or to do anything else for that matter. There was no strong emotional tie there for either one of us, and since we'd been married less than a year and had no children, it seemed that an annulment was the best path to take. Our domestic lifestyle didn't help the situation either. We had rented the first floor of what we thought was a one family home in Elmont, Long Island. What was unseen was a rear entrance to an attic apartment that at the time was occupied by a young born-again Christian married couple. When we signed the lease we were unaware that we'd have anyone living in our attic. Their close proximity made it almost impossible for us to come and go without getting into conversations and it frequently ended up with the husband, Rocky, trying to sell me a bible, or unleash a sermon that preceded the sales pitch. It wasn't until I loudly pronounced my affiliation as a born-again agnostic that the bible sales pitches ceased. It was far from a comfortable scene.

While I was spending this dreadfully forgettable period of my life, my former roommate Al had taken a furnished room in Manhattan on the upper west side. It was in an old brownstone, and the lack of air conditioning meant he slept with the unscreened window wide open, allowing pigeons to wander in onto his windowsill in the early morning. Their cooing sounds and fluttering wings would wake him at an early hour. This didn't sit well with Al, who was never meant to be an early riser. After my gaining an annulment from Frances, I had luckily obtained an apartment at the Parc Vendome, a handsome pre-war high-rise on the west side of Manhattan between west 56th and 57th Street. Once again, I extended the offer for Al to share the cost and move in. At least we'd have an air conditioner and screens. We were buddies with a common cross to bear, each with a failed marriage. The fortunate part of this arrangement was that the apartment was rent-controlled, and in New York during the mid 1950s, this was a *coup*. The rent was $108 per month, which included utilities, a switchboard, a doorman and Whyte's restaurant on the premises. Split between us it came to $54 apiece, which we could easily afford.

The Parc Vendome was a stately building with most tenants being older, long-term residents. The sudden appearance of two recently divorced guys in their twenties was not a situation the residents or the staff was used to dealing with. A few well-known celebrities resided there, among them comedian Jack E. "Fat Jack" Leonard and songwriter Johnny Burke. Whenever Burke threw a party in his penthouse I'd be invited, as I knew how to play all the songs he'd written with his partner, Jimmy Van Heusen. As for Jack E. Leonard, I'd played his act a number of times and he knew me well enough to do his usual routine of insults. At times, while waiting for the elevator, I'd hear his voice as the car neared my floor. The operator would open the door and the lone passenger would beckon to me:

"Get in here, you little cocker!" would be Leonard's opening line. I'd then have to listen to his whole comedy routine on the ride down and walking through the lobby to the street. Sometimes I'd stop by the Stage Delicatessen on my way home for a snack after a job. That's where 'Fat Jack' held court with his peers. I'd be seated across the room, and as I'd get up to pay my check, he'd yell across the room,

"Don't leave yet. Wait for me!"

He wasn't comfortable walking home alone at two o'clock in the morning and wanted company for the three-block trek. I then heard the whole comedy routine again! I must admit he was truly a funny man, so I really didn't mind waiting for him.

In the meantime Al and I both began dating again sometimes with fair results, other times not so great. However, we became notorious with the elevator operators. Whenever a single woman entered an elevator who didn't live in the building, they would automatically deposit her at our floor with a leering smirk. At the end of 1958 we both had New Years Eve jobs. Mine ended earlier than Al's, and upon returning to the

Parc Vendome I used my key to enter. It was a security building, and as I entered the lobby I found the elevator operator asleep on a couch. I woke him gently and he scrambled to his feet, then he headed toward the elevator. It took him a few tries to park the elevator at our floor, and I could see that he'd been doing a bit of celebrating while on duty. He finally got it level with the outer elevator door, and as I exited the cage I wished him a happy new year.

About an hour later, Al came in grousing about how he had to walk up to our floor. The elevator man apparently had taken a few more swigs and was totally looped! When Al got in the elevator, the elevator man had closed the inner gate but not the outer one. He held the control handle down for about fifteen seconds with his eyes shut then opened the gate. They were still in the lobby. At that point, I recall Al took it upon himself to close the doors and bring the car to our floor. As he was walking toward our apartment door, he heard scuffling back by the elevator. The operator was on the floor, half in the corridor and half in the elevator cab, obviously unable to get back to the lobby. At that point, Al turned around, took the elevator and the operator back to the lobby and proceeded to walk up to our apartment.

There was a White Tower hamburger place about a block east of where we lived, and they served tiny but tasty hamburgers twenty-four hours a day. I seem to recall that they cost fifteen cents apiece. As an added bargain, you could get an even dozen for a dollar and fifty cents. We often took advantage of the offer on the way home from late night jobs. We'd each wolf down about six of those mini-burgers complete with the pickles and fried onions that were automatic built-ins. My digestive system was pretty fair, but Al, after having slept twenty minutes would invariably bolt upright and head for the Pepto-Bismol bottle. Having come from a Mid-western background, his exposure to grease and spice had been limited. He still claims he never knew what indigestion was until he moved in with me. Over the years, Al gradually lost the Indiana dialect and has become *Mister Manhattan*. He went on to become a fixture in the New York music scene and a member of the Union Trial Board.

It was at about this time that I got my first offer to conduct for a name performer. Personal manager Tino Barzie had contacted Howie Salat, a pianist friend of mine to conduct some road dates for singer Jaye P. Morgan who he represented. For those who remember her, she was a free spirit with a bent toward kookiness. Nonetheless she had a good jazz feel and her arrangements were excellent. The charts had been done by Peter Matz and Marion Evans, and really swung. Howie was unable to take the position and recommended that Barzie get in touch with me. I accepted the offer since it was one way to do something other than club dates. After considerable time rehearsing with Ms. Morgan, we opened at the Americana Hotel in Miami. This truly was an experience for me, since I'd always been at the piano while someone else conducted. The first time in front of a band waving my arms, I kept wondering why the band got slower as I kept conducting. Little did I realize that a conductor must get the tempo in his or her head and be a few milliseconds ahead of the reaction time of the musicians. I was actually following them and they in turn were following me! This is one case where I learned my trade at the expense of Jaye P. and later a great many other performers to boot.

In the meantime Al had signed on to travel as bassist with Johnny Mathis and was on the road a great portion of the time. While he was away on tour I was contacted by an agent for a relatively unknown (to me) singer named Paul Anka. Paul was seventeen and an obvious star in the world of teenyboppers. I had never even heard the name but the salary sounded good, and I had a chance to join arranging luminaries such as Johnny Mandel and Sid Feller in writing arrangements for the act. Paul was to open at the world famous Copacabana in New York on his eighteenth birthday. In New York one had to attain that age in order to be allowed to perform anywhere that liquor was sold. Anka had to go through the same degrading mug shot and cabaret license that the rest of us had to endure. In any event I jumped at the chance since his future seemed to be limitless.

Bob with Paul Anka
Sahara Hotel, Las Vegas. 1960

Sharing the apartment worked out well for Al and me.
With both of us traveling for different artists, we weren't on
top of one another enough to get on each other's nerves. On

occasion I'd get in a huff because I'd go to the liquor cabinet for some of my Chivas Regal and find an empty bottle. Al would have finished it and forgotten to replace it. I wasn't angry with that, but Al's replacement scotch turned out to be Macy's Two Star Special, something remotely akin to Aqua Velva. That was a trigger mechanism for to me to blow my stack at Al.

The experience I gained conducting for Anka was invaluable, and the more conducting I did the more confidence I gained. However playing bubble-gum rock and tunes for teenyboppers was not especially gratifying for me. I was well past that musical stage so the overall experience felt regressive. After spending about a year and a half with Anka, I was approached by Johnny Mathis' manager who had gotten my name from Al. The offer sounded good and it was another stepping stone to something higher in the music industry, or so I thought. I gave notice to Irvin Feld, Anka's manager and soon after received a plane ticket to Los Angeles. It came from Mathis' manager, Helen Noga, a noted hard-nosed tyrant, which made me think twice about my choice. However I felt that this change could provide an insight into the Hollywood scene.

For the past few years, I had been exceptionally intrigued with a form of jazz that had evolved in L.A. with giants such as Gerry Mulligan, Shorty Rogers and Marty Paitch. They were making one L.P. after another of well-arranged *cool* sounds. This was labeled as *West Coast jazz*, and was at odds with the seemingly structureless jazz that was at the time prevalent in New York. Here was my chance to see what it was all about.

My arrival in Los Angeles was less than auspicious. Not all airliners were jet powered in those days, and I was on a DC-6 four-engine prop job. It took about ten hours to fly coast-to-coast so I settled in as best I could. Upon takeoff the stewardess (this was before the politically correct term *Flight Attendant* was in vogue) offered chewing gum to the passengers. I gladly accepted and within ten minutes, a large filling in one of my rear molars had been yanked out and was imbedded in the Chiclets. It was a Saturday and we weren't scheduled to land until late evening. I knew there would not be an available dentist late at night, or the next day for that matter. I tried to chew on the other side of my mouth, not drink anything too hot or too cold and accept the discomfort. There weren't any options.

I was booked by the Mathis organization at the Hotel Wilcox, a run down fleabag in a seedy part of Hollywood. The car, furnished by the Mathis group, turned out to be a twelve-year-old Oldsmobile torpedo-back with its best miles long gone. This was only the beginning of a classic mismatch between artist, artist's manager and conductor. At the first rehearsal I found a troupe of male "gypsies," a term used for freelance dancers, that were part of the new Mathis show. There was also a choreographer, Hermes Pan who was renowned for his work with Fred Astaire. This was all new to me, since I'd never been exposed to production shows with an entire cast of participants. I'd been doing okay as a personal conductor and accompanist, but this new challenge loomed larger than life, and to be honest I was terrified. The Limelighters, a folk singing group who were popular at the time, had also been included on the bill.

After gratefully finding a dentist whose hands reeked of cigar smoke to replace the errant filling, I started a rehearsal schedule with the upcoming Mathis tour group. My heart wasn't in it, and to boot I had many negative words with Helen Noga, Johnny's manager. Helen was notorious in the industry, almost dwarfish in stature, having a longshoreman's vocabulary and all the charm of an underfed piranha. Just about any sensible request from me was usually met with, "F—k you, Honey." It didn't take me too many days to realize that I wasn't going to be particularly happy with this venture. We did a few local one-nighters in the western part of the country, and during that time I really got the feeling that this career move was not a positive one. I never bonded with Johnny or anyone else in the organization, nor did I feel that I would ever fit. I wasn't ready to take on the responsibility of conducting a production of the magnitude that they had prepared, and I felt more depressed every day that I worked with the choreographer and the dancers. I didn't know exactly why, but it was a gut feeling. I decided to honor that feeling.

After discussing the situation with Al Hood I gave Helen Noga my notice, and two weeks later was aboard a plane headed back to New York, this time refusing the offer of gum.

My conducting days continued with an offer to go with Jane Morgan, (not to be confused with Jaye P.) to the Radisson Hotel in Minneapolis. Jane was a chanteuse best known for her hit record of "Fascination." Her vocal style was to blithely float the melody without ever establishing a sense of the tempo she desired. She was not what I'd call a swinging singer and although her meter was there, her sense of time was not exactly akin to Ella Fitzgerald. As a result this pretty much left it up to the conductor to guess where she wanted the tempo to be. Wherever my guesses happened to land, they apparently weren't anywhere near her desired tempos. She would wait in the wings after each performance, eyes bulging and face reddening, poised to tell me everything I did wrong. At the time, she was married to former chorus boy Laurence Stith, to whom she allotted a couple of solo vocal numbers within her act. On the rare occasion when Jane was satisfied that I didn't sabotage her selections, Laurence would throw a snit and tell me that this particular night I'd loused up his numbers. We happened to have a hotel band that was not very show-savvy with a rhythm section that Guy Lombardo would have been delighted to have. In an effort to save the engagement, I suggested she fly out a couple of rhythm players from New York and try to shore up the band. She did, and it still didn't help. My resentment toward her grew with each performance

Jane's opening number was one of those *I'm happy you're here, and I love everybody* type of specially written songs, which she sang while gliding from table to table at the edge of the floor, shaking hands with the various patrons. One night while doing this piece of special material at the Radisson Hotel's Flame Room in Minneapolis, an inebriated patron reached out to shake her hand, simultaneously erupting into a projectile vomit, all highlighted by a spotlight. I should have controlled my reaction, but I didn't. I simply doubled over with laughter and couldn't even continue playing the piano part! Needless to say this, too, did not sit well with Ms. Morgan. The tension built, and shortly thereafter we had a mutual parting of the ways. Ordinarily I would handle my business dealings with courtesy and aplomb but not in this case. I had gone to the hotel bar after the show and had enough scotch to feel that I could fully express myself. I knocked on Jane's hotel room door. She answered in her nightgown with a caustic,

"Well, what is it?"

"I hate this town, your show is shitty and you stink! I quit!" With that I stormed down the hallway toward my hotel room and began to pack. It was not the way I would ever choose to end a business relationship, and I still have regrets that I lost control.

Back to the union floor, and the club date scene!

CHAPTER 9

WESTWARD HO!

After spending the next year or so doing more club dates, I began to abhor the disregard for musicality. Leaders would hire a singer and hand him an old plywood bass that had been painted white. It may have had only two or possibly three strings attached to the tuning pegs, and it's doubtful anyone ever gave thought to trying to tune it. It wouldn't have made much difference since these singers were told to simply pluck the strings and make it look as if they knew how to play. The singing was the feature the leaders wanted. To most of them a bass, even when played well sounded like another bass drum.

The drummers were equally as bad. Most were related either by blood or marriage to the leader, or they were cronies from bygone years. There was no such thing as musical taste on any of these jobs. These lead-footed, hammer-handed hockers sounded like a steel factory at full output. The fact was we were a factory; A music factory that ground out one tune after another with little or no regard for correct chords or any subtle musical innuendos. Despite the financial rewards it was becoming increasingly difficult to maintain a positive attitude.

Having been to Los Angeles and having had some experience with the music scene there at the time, I began entertaining thoughts of moving. I had done a few television shows in New York, just getting one foot in the door, but it soon became apparent that the television industry was moving to

Los Angeles. The problem seemed to be twofold: Space in New York was tight for prop storage and the theatres were small. The second reason was based upon the talent pool of stars. Los Angeles was home to over ninety percent of them.

I toyed with this idea through about three heavy snowstorms in the winter of 1959-1960. On a less conscious level, I think I'd made up my mind that I was going but hadn't decided exactly when. After the third major snowfall I couldn't find my car, an English Ford convertible called a *Consul.* The snowplows had heaped piles of slush and soot-stained snow on top of all the cars parked curbside rendering each of them as part of a massive snowdrift. About six days went by before I could identify my car, which by now had no top. The weight of the snow had collapsed it. This was the catalyst that would finally propel my trip westward.

I informed Al Hood that I'd be taking leave of the *Big Apple* in about three weeks, and we worked out a deal whereby he bought my remaining furnishings. At this point in his life, he'd met Lillian, a great lady who would shortly become his second wife. The apartment at the Parc Vendome would be of great advantage, at least temporarily for the two of them. I packed most of my belongings in cartons and an old steamer trunk and shipped them out to a drummer friend, Allen Goodman who had recently moved to Los Angeles. The phone rang while I was settling up my accounts in New York and having a new top put on the Consul. It was Julie Wilson, famed chanteuse and all-around great lady with whom I had worked previously in my career. She'd booked ten days in Miami and asked if I'd be her accompanist. After figuring out the logistics, I realized that it was possible to drive to Florida, do Julie's job and then head cross-country to Los Angeles. Since I had no particular time frame in which to coordinate my move, I accepted Julie's offer. Musicians learn early in the music business never to decline an offer of work. This was no exception, even though it would take me about thirteen hundred miles away from my pre-planned route.

We spent a pleasant ten days at one of the Collins Avenue

hotels in Miami Beach. It was uneventful except for my own anxiety at the immensity of the planned move to Los Angeles. When we finished the engagement, I bade Julie farewell and started off in my underpowered vehicle for California. The *Consul* felt as if six mice on a treadmill powered it. Fortunately I didn't have a lot of excess luggage, since I'd dumped the accordion in the East River upon leaving New York. At that time there weren't many interstate highways, so it meant traveling through small towns and speed traps. I didn't have a great deal of money for this move, and that made it riskier. There were small motels and cabins en route with lots of barbeque joints nearby. I was doing okay until somewhere in Missouri my fan belt broke. The Ford dealer there had never heard of a *Consul*, and had nothing that would fit the tiny four-cylinder motor. I was in a quandary as to how to resolve the problem. I noticed a nearby appliance store and found that a belt for a washing machine was an adequate size to replace the original. The car ran, but I now realized that pretty soon I'd be heading through the Rockies and later the desert. Without a great deal of confidence in the car the results could be problematic. I found a used car lot, and negotiated the sale of my car for the price of a one-way airline ticket from St. Joseph, Missouri to Los Angeles. For the remainder of the trip I was airborne and the next day, suitcase in tow, I landed in Los Angeles with Allen & Beverly Goodman waiting to pick me up.

I believe I had about seven hundred dollars and an American Express card when Los Angeles became my new residence. Allen drove me around apartment hunting, and I eventually settled for an apartment on Sycamore Avenue in Hollywood, one block behind Graumann's Chinese Theatre. It was in a three story building on a tree-lined street with the quintessential swimming pool in the center. I had an efficiency apartment with a full kitchen and the rent was $125 per month. The utilities were included except for a telephone, which I immediately had installed. For a musician, a phone was the pipeline to work. An answering service was another necessity.

My next step was buying a car. I found a used fire engine

red 1957 Plymouth with tail fins but minus a first gear for $250. Once I learned to take off from a standing stop in second gear, it ran fine. It got me to the musicians union on Vine Street where I paid my initiation fee and listened to the mandatory initiation pep talk from one of the union officials. At that time a new member couldn't leave the jurisdiction for six months and had to check in to the union headquarters once a week in person. At last I was somewhere that the local populace paid attention to musical quality, or so I thought.

The first call I had was from Barney Sorkin, a society leader. Needing whatever funds I could earn I took the call despite misgivings since it was essentially just another club date. A west coast Lester Lanin I thought, jokingly. I arrived in ample time to meet the other players, who I'd known by reputation. Former Stan Kenton bassist Don Bagley and drummer Frank DeVito from the Buddy DeFranco quintet comprised the rhythm section. These were great musicians and now I knew I had broken the cycle of horrible rhythm sections I'd been partnered with in New York. The unknown element was Barney Sorkin. In came Barney, dressed impeccably, smiling, and very affable. He introduced himself, said he was happy that I could work with him, and proceeded to count off the first tune with his alto sax in hand. I played the obligatory four bar introduction and Barney started to play "Some Enchanted Evening." I have never in my life heard a sound like his emanate from a musical instrument. The best way I can describe it was a cross between a goose clucking and a mouse peeing on a blotter! It was a 1920s sound that I may have heard on an old 78 record and joked about. I thought he was putting us on, and I started to chuckle. Bagley leaned over and said,

"Don't laugh, he's for real."

The humor quickly faded from my dazed and confused mind. My next thought was, "What have I done? I came twenty-five hundred miles to get away from this kind of non-music and this was my reward." Nonetheless, it was a matter of financial necessity, so I bit my lip and got through the night. Barney generously rewarded us at the end of the engagement, then he asked if I could do a date with him the following week. I agreed. Little did I know the date was to be in New York! Some wealthy lady from New York was flying Barney and the entire band back to play her party at the Westchester Country Club. So, not only was I still faced with grinding out the club date music that I despised, but also I had to return to the area that I'd just left, hoping that I'd never see it again.

Barney had his own idea about what dance music should be. Once when we were playing "Some Enchanted Evening," obviously one of Barney's favorites, I started to play my chorus and heard Barney singing to Frank DeVito, to the tune,

"Softer on the bass drum...Lighter on the cymbal...That's the way to play it....If you want to work for me...."

At least the rent got paid on the Sycamore apartment and I got home in time to make my weekly appearance at union headquarters. Allen Goodman, who also recently moved to L.A., was in the same unfortunate situation of not being well connected in the music business. A third New York friend, Mort Klanfer and his wife Geri had also recently migrated, and we all had our sights set on the television music industry. Meanwhile we were scuffling. Money was so tight we'd often get together, pool some cash and make a big vat of pasta and a salad for basic sustenance.

While sitting around the pool at Sycamore Arms one afternoon, I met a young lady who also had a studio apartment and was in similar straits financially. After getting to know one another on a few dates, we agreed to share an apartment. If we moved up to a one-bedroom place in the same building it would be $160 per month, which meant we'd each contribute $80 instead of the $125 each had been shelling out. Also, one phone would do for the both of us since we weren't prone to overly long phone tie-ups. This worked out to our mutual advantage for a few months, until one day her estranged husband came by to try reconciliation. He was an airman and although I never met him, I heard that he wore size sixteen shoes and was six-feet six-inches tall. She agreed to go back with him and our relationship ended as abruptly as it began. From the description, I think it was best that I never did meet him.

By the time I had put in my six months and gotten my union card, things still weren't happening the way I'd hoped. I was primarily working club dates and making ends meet, but that was not what I'd hoped to accomplish in Los Angeles. I had to consider making some changes even if it meant moving again, albeit not part of the original master plan. Fortunately, I received an offer to go to Las Vegas for thirteen weeks as pianist-conductor for the De Castro Sisters, three Cuban ladies who had a Vegas lounge act and a recent hit record of "Teach Me Tonight." The salary was $500 a week. At this point my decision was purely for financial benefit. I accepted the offer, then packed my record albums, stereo system and clothing in the old red Plymouth, paid up my last month's rent at Sycamore Arms and set off to the next adventure: Las Vegas.

CHAPTER 10

GLITTER GULCH

The Las Vegas of 1961 was an entirely different town than the one that exists today. It had a population of 60,000 residents, and the highest building in town was the Riviera Hotel on the strip, which was about eight stories. Most of the strip hotels were two stories high and sprawling complexes with large glamorous pools in the center. The space between hotels was nothing but sand interspersed with occasional souvenir shops. There was one traffic signal between Sahara Avenue and McCarren Airport, which sat at the far end of the strip. The airline service consisted of Bonanza Airlines, and an occasional flight from United, depositing passengers on the tarmac. Arriving passengers were greeted with hot desert winds while inside the terminal rows of mechanical slot machines whirred their noisy wheels while being played by jackpot hopefuls. In contrast, today's Las Vegas airport is larger than the entire town of Las Vegas was back then.

While still living in New York, I had played the Sahara in Las Vegas with Paul Anka in what was probably the worst booking faux pas of the decade. Paul, age eighteen at the time was paired with Sophie Tucker who was in her waning years. Rather than attract both generations, the combination repelled both seniors and juniors. The younger set was not allowed to come and see Anka because of Tucker's reputed "blue" material. The older set wouldn't sit through forty-five minutes of a teen idol to see Tucker's adult presentation. The result was a string of nearly empty houses. Chalk up a big demerit for then house-booker Stan Irwin. The only benefit was that I had some idea of what Las Vegas was all about, and I knew that there was a plethora of entertainment venues with a shortage of good pianists.

I was pleasantly surprised to find here some of the finest jazz all-stars who I had known by reputation. Among them were trombonist Carl Fontana, and multi-instrumentalist Bob Enevoldsen, playing both valve trombone and tenor sax. We played on a revolving stage in the Stardust lounge, opposite Mexican pianist-arranger Esquivel. The thirteen week engagement stretched to twenty-six, and I began to get a good reputation around Las Vegas.

At the time there weren't many places for me to rent a furnished apartment. The selection was the Robinson Apartments, the Blair House, the Bali Ha'i and the Country Club apartments. In the course of my stay, I lived in all of them at one point or another. While at the Blair House at about three A.M. one summer night, the central air conditioning unit in my apartment failed. The place became a sauna, and in my desperation I hauled the mattress from the bed onto the grassy front lawn, and proceeded to go to sleep under the stars. This was all well and good, except that the lawn sprinklers were on a timer set for five-thirty A.M. Needless to say the result was a true awakening, and a wet one at that!

My thirteen-week stay turned into a two-year engagement as I shifted from the Stardust to the Sands Hotel lounge, where I headed the backup quartet that played for nearly every artist performing at that venue. Jerry Vale was a lounge act back then, and I played for him during his appearances at the Sands. It was a great time in the city of neon. The hotel guests were well dressed, finely coiffed and exuded glamour, especially on weekends when the glitterati from Hollywood would descend upon the town. The ladies-of-the-evening would sip a cocktail at the bar waiting for some anxious John to approach them or for a message from a bellman who was the liaison between a guest and the desired prey. The Sands lounge drew its share of celebrities. Frank Sinatra, Sammy Davis Jr., Dean Martin and other luminaries were regular showroom performers at that hotel, and they drew a big Hollywood contingent, many of whom would spill over into the lounge

Around this time, the marriage of Louis Prima and Keely Smith had come to an end. Keely had been replaced by singer Gia Scala, later to become Louis' second wife. Keely was about to embark on a showroom act of her own, and she approached me to take on the task of musical director. The money sounded good, and I'd just about had enough of the lounge work. I accepted the position and went into rehearsal with Keely and company.

It was a wild time in my life, and I made my share of mistakes while living there. I found that other than a couple of musician buddies, the town was a veritable desert, not only in terrain but also in emotional humanity. It drew people who were attracted to the fast money, and had little regard for anything other than the almighty buck. Nearly everyone I met had one or more of the three major character flaws that made Vegas an unstable community: Drinking, gambling or spousal cheating. The town lent itself to all of those vices. Not being a gambler, that didn't affect me. Being single, my liaisons couldn't be classified as cheating. I did however imbibe a bit. Martinis were the cocktails of choice, and I had more than my share. This led to one disaster when I awoke one morning hung over, then finding a marriage license on the dresser of my apartment showing that at four-thirty A.M., I had exchanged vows at City Hall with a lady I barely knew who was still asleep in my bed.

When the sickness and the blue fumes had cleared, we realized that this was a huge mistake. She was a lovely lady who was there to spend her six-week residency in order to obtain her divorce, as the Nevada law allowed back then. She had an eight-year-old son, and my being a person who shares W. C. Fields' view of children, this didn't sit too well with me. A quick annulment followed, and at that time I swore off martinis, a vow to which I adhere until this day. Scotch...well, that's another matter.

If Keely Smith had one flaw in her stage show it was the inability to control her blathering. She made certain to broadcast my indiscretion at each show, to a full audience. When the news of my blooper hit the Las Vegas show-biz columns, it became the talk of the town. I decided it would be prudent to lay low for a while. I took off to Los Angeles and spent a couple of weeks waiting for the gossip to cool down. Los Angeles was where I had intended to live, and this debacle merely drove home that fact. All the time I was living in Las Vegas, I'd been booking occasional recording sessions in L.A. and commuting back and forth. By this time, my red Plymouth had made the trip to the bone yard and I had purchased an attractive Volkswagen Karmann-Ghia. It was a tan sports coupe that still had the VW engine but was slightly souped up with a Porsche kit. What that did was add some sorely needed extra horsepower. In 1961 Interstate 15 had not yet been built, and the road between Las Vegas and L.A. was a two-lane job with a lot of truck traffic. There was the infamous Baker Grade, a thirteen-mile climb on a seven-degree angle, which would bring the ascending truck traffic to a crawl. A VW with a normal engine wouldn't stand a chance in hell of passing on that hill, but the Porsche kit gave me an advantage. In second gear with the accelerator jammed to the floor, I could conceivably get past an occasional semi. However, the Karmann-Ghia had no air-conditioning, and in the hundred and twenty degree summers it made for a less than comfortable seven-hour drive. The town of Yermo was the halfway point between Los Angeles and Las Vegas, and it was my refueling stop. Then I'd continue motoring on through desert peaks and valleys. It was a long trip under the best of circumstances, and to amuse myself I often fantasized that I'd come across a love-starved young ingénue who was stranded along the roadside. Regretfully that never happened. As I neared Las Vegas, the towns preceding it were Blue Diamond and Pahrump. The name Pahrump always made me chuckle as it resembled the phonetic sound of an elephant's flatulation. I had worked at the Nugget Hotel in Sparks, Nevada where Bertha, the trained elephant performed.

If anyone has ever walked by the backside of an elephant that was passing wind at the moment, one can fully understand my word association. Pah-**rump!**

Keely had a female manager by the name of Barbara Belle who was probably close to six feet tall, about two hundred pounds, and shared a kinship with Helen Noga, Johnny Mathis' manager. She, too, was a difficult person to deal with, having the vocabulary of a longshoreman. Keely's act was to involve a group of ten dancers, all of whom would wear Keely wigs with the jet-black pageboy-and-bangs hairdo. A great deal of time and effort was put into the production, and in about three months time we opened at the Riviera in Vegas. I inherited drummer Bobby Morris, the one member of the Louis-Keely lounge group who had defected to the Keely camp. We co-existed as team workers but never bonded as friends. Bobby was a different type of personality than I was, and our differences made it easier to stay a fair distance from one another. Bobby felt that he had worked with Keely longer than me and that he knew more about her than I ever would. That was all true, but as conductor my job was to lead the entire orchestra. Bobby would never accept the tempos that I would indicate. He'd intentionally look the other direction, away from the piano where I was situated, and loudly carry the band in whatever direction he thought it should go. This made for a rather rag-tag imprecise sound on many occasions and led to a great many arguments between the two of us.

Six months later while traveling with the Keely show, we played the Cocoanut Grove in Hollywood at the Ambassador Hotel. Dick Stabile, who was the former conductor for Dean Martin and Jerry Lewis was the house orchestra leader there. I must have impressed him because he offered me the job as house pianist, should I ever want to accept. This set me thinking: This could be my entree into the Los Angeles scene. I kept that thought in mind as I continued on with Keely playing Chicago, Philadelphia, Cherry Hill, New Jersey and New York. I decided the time was right to call it quits when at the Americana Hotel in New York City I encountered another

Lester Lanin band hired as the house orchestra to play the show. I knew the guys from my early days playing club dates and despite their great repertoire of dance tunes, they were poor readers and had a terrible time playing any show. The hotel management didn't understand my complaints about the orchestral personnel since they had hired them purely on the Lester Lanin name. The fact that they played good dance music but didn't read worth a damn was beyond the hotel manager's comprehension. It became a big brouhaha with Ms. Smith, Ms. Belle and the choreographer. It was one hassle too many. I gave my notice, went back to Las Vegas just long enough to pack the Karmann-Ghia with whatever it would hold, and headed back to rent an apartment in L.A. By this time, I'd squirreled away enough to hold me if times got tough, so with an air of confidence I found an apartment on Rossmore Avenue. Vegas still held a fascination, but I knew that I couldn't exist for very long in that environment. Now I had to see what life in L.A. held in store for my musical future.

DICK STABILE ORCH., 1963

CHAPTER 11

"HOORAY FOR HOLLYWOOD"

To a person from New York, Hollywood had a mystique that was not easy to define. New York City was grays, blacks, vacant stares and pedestrian paranoia. Hollywood was palm trees, pastel colors and mini-skirts. At least that's the way it was in 1963. Starlets with flowing blond locks cavorted around the town in MGs and Austin Healey sports cars wearing see-through blouses. It was a bachelor's ultimate fantasy. The feeling wouldn't last too long, especially when I began to sense the underbelly of what was really transpiring. In reality the city was a gritty place within a movie set façade. Even the palm trees were not native. They were imported from other countries by the early developers of Hollywood.

The view from the terrace of my apartment on Rossmore Avenue overlooked a golf course. On the front side I faced a seven-story apartment known as The Ravenswood, which was owned by the notoriously bawdy sex symbol Mae West. Still alive at the time, she occupied the entire top floor with her parade of young studs entering and exiting at all hours of the day and night. Rossmore Avenue was an extension of Vine Street, and I lived only three blocks away from the Hollywood musicians union. I should have had a clue that the town was a bit off-center when one of my neighbors at the Rossmore apartment kept knocking on my door and wanting to come in for coffee while her husband, a burly stagehand was at work at Columbia Studios. She had amorous intentions, but I was not about to be a taker, having seen the muscular frame of her spouse. I didn't have a death wish, and still don't.

In the ensuing months, I found a job as the leader of the house trio at a joint on La Cienega Boulevard called the Trolley-Ho. One of the performers was Lenny Bruce, who was busted in one of his many arrests for the use of profane language. The featured singer on the bill with Mr. Bruce was a young Hispanic girl of eighteen named Vikki Carr. I accompanied her both at the Trolley-Ho and the Crescendo on Sunset Strip before her rapid rise to stardom. One of her trademarks besides having a good voice was her ability to cry on cue, which she did to excess nightly. She had a good set of pipes, and I knew she'd become a star in the very near future.

The house booking agent was a woman named Sally Marr who happened to be Lenny Bruce's mother. In her early days she had been a striptease artist with a somewhat checkered past, but in deciding to go straight she took to booking up-and-coming comedians. One young Japanese stand-up comic was destined to go on to fame as a movie actor in many feature films. Pat Morita starred in "The Karate Kid" as well as many other film and television productions. I spent a good period of time at the Trolley-Ho but the paychecks were getting rather iffy, as they were delayed more often than not. Eventually they started to bounce so my eyes turned toward other possible venues of work.

Another club on La Cienega Boulevard featured Bobby Troup and his trio six nights a week. Bobby was a pianist/singer/songwriter who at the time was married to the beautiful and sensuous vocalist Julie London. I had befriended Bobby's bassist, former Stan Kenton alumnus Don Bagley, who at the time bore an uncanny resemblance to me. People often mistook us for brothers although "Bags" as he was known, was somewhat slimmer than me. I'd pop in periodically to hear the group and got acquainted with Bobby along with his guitarist John Gray. Bobby had gotten bored with the small turnout on weekdays and decided he only would play on weekends. He asked me if I'd like to play in his place on Tuesdays, Wednesdays and Thursdays which is a musician's dream. Those are usually the slowest days of the week since our work usually tends toward weekend gigs. This led to my meeting a lot more of the west coast stalwarts, musicians who made a name for themselves in the heyday of the "birth of the cool" phase of jazz. They were all good connections, and they spread my name amongst their circle of contemporaries.

Just about this time the notorious Playboy Club opened its doors on Sunset Strip, and I was asked lead one of three trios to play in what was known as *the living room*. It was the heyday of the posh and the plush, the utmost of luxury and elegance. I managed to end up playing the weekends there while still filling in for Troup on the weekdays. Being a young bachelor the environment of shapely young ladies in bunny costumes was nirvana. Although today it would be considered politically incorrect to have such a setup, back in the early 60s it was certainly part of the culture. The *bunnies* were forbidden to socialize with other employees outside the premises, so that took an element of possible excitement away from the equation. However, that rule didn't extend to the director of personnel, a former "bunny" who had her own agenda set toward me.

Another place of employment was Dino's, a Sunset Strip restaurant allegedly owned by Dean Martin. Although I never saw Dean in or around the establishment, his brother was a greeter at the door for a period of time. The music was a piano and bass duo situated in front of a massive stone fireplace, and there was always a featured female singer. Some of these ingénues were noteworthy, while others had ascended in their respective careers via the casting couch or in some cases, any old couch.

Pianists had a great appeal to these wannabees since we could provide needed services, such as playing auditions, writing arrangements and accompanying them at clubs where they were booked. They would be more than happy to bestow their womanly favors on me if I met the aforementioned criteria. This type of bartering began to wear thin after awhile, as the main topics day or night were their career, what their agent was going to do for them and how they looked forward to becoming a star. Happily, I was only the off-night sub at Dino's, which allowed me to escape much of the Hollywood ingénue prattle. I did a great deal of job-hopping at the time because there was a plethora of work during the sixties in Los Angeles, and it was refreshing to bounce from one environment to another. There were numerous performers appearing worldwide who were in constant need of a traveling pianist/conductor, and the salaries were attractive. As a pianist/conductor I had to be in rehearsals and attend meetings, be the librarian for the artist's music, and often a hand-servant for the artist's ego. The position did have certain built-in perks, and I quickly learned how to use them to my advantage.

Jet planes had not yet become common conveyances, and most flights were still on DC-6 prop aircraft. The planes were slow, lumbering aircraft that turned a cross-country flight into a ten-hour ordeal. Often I'd end up on a "red-eye" flight from New York to Los Angeles. The payload of passengers was relatively small in comparison to the jumbo jets of today. Often a late flight would have only thirty passengers, most of whom were stretched out across two seats, covered by a blanket and hoping to wake up in time for breakfast just prior to landing. There were usually three or four flight attendants on an aircraft, and in those days the requirements to fill those positions were for cute and shapely young females. I figured out that if I were to take an all-night flight, I could sleep the day before and be able to stay up all night and shmooze with the ladies in the semi-circular lounge. Many of them were fascinated with the idea of my connection with a pop idol of the day, so I'd graciously extend an invitation to be my guest at one of the shows. This allowed me to collect phone numbers and future dates with some very cute young ladies. I always was a sucker for girls in uniform!

Getting back to my job-hopping days in Los Angeles. Across the street from the aforementioned Trolley-Ho was a club built into a storefront owned by and named after two siblings, the Slate Brothers, who had been bit players in the film industry. I ended up as house pianist at that club that featured comedian Redd Foxx, vocalist Damita Jo and a young singer, Jack Jones. I have always loved accompanying and I'd usually get along quite well with singers. Jack Jones was no exception. At the time, he had a number of hits on the charts "Wives & Lovers," "A Lot of Livin' to Do," "Call Me Irresponsible" were just a few. He extended an offer for me to be his conductor on the road with the first stop being Sydney, Australia. That was a chance I couldn't pass up, so I signed on. Aside from the prestige of being Jack's musical director, the thought of a twenty-two hour flight with cute ladies in uniform was something I eagerly anticipated. I was never so disappointed. The attendants were all males on that Qantas flight! Oh well, there was always scotch.

Sydney proved to be a young bachelor's dream. At the time women outnumbered men five to one, and the gals loved American males. The average Australian male's priorities were 1) football, 2) beer and 3) women. Most American men favored #3 in the #1 spot, so the ladies were overly attracted to any male who arrived from the United States. Needless to say my days were well taken up with romantic adventures, and my nights weren't too bad either!

Appearing at a nearby nightclub was Don Cornell, a romantic crooner from the '50s. I became friendly with Jack Holliday, his conductor who hailed from Las Vegas. Jack was formerly with a novelty group called *the Goofers* that made numerous appearances on variety shows such as Ed Sullivan. We immediately struck up a friendship that would last until his untimely demise in 1974. I'm still very close with his widow, Joy, who is a unique and terrific lady. Cornell was appearing at a nightclub called *Checkers* that was owned by Dennis Wong, a ne'er-do-well from Hong Kong. Dennis was the epitome of *Murphy's Law*. Whatever endeavor he undertook could and **did** go wrong. Dennis' father in Hong Kong financed his business ventures in Australia, probably to keep him there and out of his hair.

Dennis was notorious for his misadventures. It was around

this time The Beatles came upon the pop music scene and Dennis, not wanting to be left behind, ventured to England to audition them. At the end of the presentation, he asked about the cost of hiring them. Somewhat taken aback by the immensity of the booking cost for the "Fab Four," he asked,

"How much for two?"

It goes without saying the Beatles never appeared at Checkers. Dennis though, was not to place second in the Sydney nightclub scene. A trip to Las Vegas gave him the idea of doing an ice show on stage. He hired a choreographer, a bunch of statuesque female skaters, and prepared his version of "Australia on Ice." This venture failed due mainly to lack of proper refrigeration, and no runoff troth at the edge of the stage. As the show progressed the ice melted rapidly and the resulting water cascaded off the end of the stage onto the patrons at ringside. The skaters were falling all over each other due to spots where the ice had completely melted, and a general sense of chaos prevailed.

Norman Erskine was the crude yet genial master of ceremonies who oversaw the fiascos that Dennis would initiate as entrepreneur. If an audience member would become boisterous, Norman would yell, "Calm yer face!" Once while Don Cornell was on stage singing, the right leg of the grand piano collapsed tilting the piano at an awkwardly oblique angle to one side. Without a moment's hesitation, Jack Holliday got down on his right knee and continued to play Don's music for the remainder of the act, hamming it up as only Jack could. He was confronted by Dennis at the end of the act, who in his inimitable dialect, told Jack,

"You do velly unplofessional show!"

Memories are made of scenes such as these!

Bob With Singer Jack Jones,
1964

CHAPTER 12

THE L.A. SCENE

The next couple of years would prove to be some of the most adventurous and important ones of my career. I can't be sure of the chronological accuracy of the events, but during the next two years I had opportunities to play many renowned establishments with many fine Los Angeles musicians. Aside from the Trolley-Ho, Slate Brothers, Dino's (of "77 Sunset Strip" fame,) I also played at the Crescendo, The Interlude and the world-famous Cocoanut Grove, the latter with Dick Stabile's orchestra.

It was an active time for live music. Almost every dining and drinking establishment had a duo or trio, or at least a pianist. Famed ex-Benny Goodman pianist Johnny Guarneri held forth in the San Fernando Valley's 'Tail of the Cock' restaurant. In Studio City Page Cavanaugh had an eight-piece group with longtime Les Brown drummer Jack Sperling heading the rhythm section. At any given spot one could see luminaries such as Pete Jolly, who had an almost endless run at Sherry's on Crescent Heights Boulevard where the famed Sunset Strip began.

Female vocalists were also employed at a number of clubs. Some of them such as Vikki Carr had great potential. Others were less talented vocally but looked good enough to draw customers. Some were wannabee starlets with limited or no talent. Their favors to the club owners usually got them the singing job. Nevertheless the nightlife was active enough to support a great diversity of entertainment.

I was fortunate to have met Steve Allen, the late great TV personality in my wanderings in Southern California. Steve was a great wit and humorist, well known for his literate spoofs and wordplay. One day while I was waiting for a flight at Los Angeles International Airport, I met up with Steve who was also heading out for a personal appearance. As we chatted, he spoke about the misuse of the English language. I then facetiously cited the title of the old Guy Lombardo recording of "Boo-Hoo." My theory was that to be grammatically correct, the title should have been "Boo-Whom." Steve replied that it should have gone one step further, and have been called "Boom-Whom." We managed to have a half an hour of good laughs between us until his flight was ready for boarding.

Steve had previously hired me as a music transcriber. He was a prolific composer and as far as I know, he had more compositions listed with ASCAP than any other composer in history. Steve would always keep a tape recorder handy in his office atop his spinet piano, and as a musical idea would pop into his head he'd turn on the tape recorder and proceed to sing and play the newly inspired song. The recorder was an old Wollensak reel-to-reel model, which by the standards of that time was state-of—the-art. About once a week a messenger would arrive at my home with a full tape of Steve's newly composed songs for me to transcribe. Steve was musically illiterate and could neither read nor write music. My job was to listen to each song, and measure-by-measure put the correct notation along with lyrics on music paper so he could register the composition with ASCAP for purposes of future royalties. This was a weekly occurrence and each time a tape would reach my desk, I'd have another dozen or so songs to notate. In my own opinion, most of the material was rather banal, using clichés of the "moon-june-spoon" variety, but a few classics evolved over time.

Steve never turned down a chance to play the piano. If he were a guest at a house party where I'd been hired as background music pianist, I would always welcome his presence. He would invariably saunter over to the piano to ask if he could play something. Once he was seated at the keyboard he was there for the duration of the evening, making my job quite simple. Not everyone shared the idea that Steve was a great pianist. Among his detractors was Hollywood curmudgeon and actor/ pianist Oscar Levant. Once while being interviewed, Oscar was asked what he though of Steve Allen's piano playing. Without missing a beat, Oscar said,

"He flits over the keys with arthritic abandon!"

All of that aside, Steve did as much to promote jazz and good music on television as anyone could have done, and on the original Tonight Show introduced singers such as Steve Lawrence, Eydie Gorme and Andy Williams. Many, myself included, miss his wit and zaniness.

Around this time my mother was starting to date Joseph Von Rottkay, a sometime binge drinker who had recently been widowed. They had met at General Motors New York offices where she had been employed as a liaison for overseas executives. When an overseas G.M. VIP would want a special item (such as dog-food) sent to Brazil, mother would take care of the request. Joe was an assistant comptroller, and not especially well-liked due to his miserable disposition when he'd been drinking. Nonetheless they found each other, and became "enablers" in their alcoholic scene. As hard as I tried throughout my later years, I could never understand her taste in men friends. My mother seemed drawn to the type that can only be described as cornball life-of-the-party conventioneers. She could not fathom why I never warmed up to any of them with their happy, backslapping insensitivity.

Meanwhile, as I was finishing up a season at the Cocoanut Grove with Dick Stabile's orchestra, singer/dancer Donald O'Connor was the last act to appear before the room closed for the summer. We seemed to hit it off well, and he asked if I'd be willing to travel on his summer tour as conductor. Donald had a book show and I thought it was a great opportunity to learn how to conduct a different format. (A book show is one that is similar to a Broadway show. It entails a complete story from beginning to end with cast members as opposed to a vocal songfest.) I accepted, and we played Las Vegas, Lake Tahoe, and Atlantic City. Part of our show included Irene Ryan, ("Granny" of "The Beverly Hillbillies") and the Wellingtons, a folk trio of collegiate lads. We had a nice camaraderie on the summer tour, and at the end, I began looking around Los Angeles to see what my next job might be.

The television season had just begun, and Jerry Lewis had been signed to do a variety show at ABC. The old El Capitan Theatre on Vine Street had been remodeled and made into a state-of-the-art television studio. As networks are prone to do, they ballyhooed this show to the moon as the greatest show ever devised. The audiences thought differently, and as the first thirteen-week cycle was nearing an end Lewis was cancelled. In order to fill the spot, the executives at ABC called upon Nick Vanoff and Bill Harbach to come up with a variety replacement. They had been producers of the Colgate Comedy Hour, The Perry Como Show, and The Steve Allen Show and were well respected in the variety show genre.

Nick and Bill's new baby "The Hollywood Palace" was set to be a TV version of the Palace Theatre in New York featuring rotating hosts, with name guest stars, and even circus acts as part of the weekly performances. It was done with class and rivaled the Ed Sullivan Show in content. The first host was Bing Crosby, the following week it was Milton Berle and the third week Donald O'Connor. One evening my phone rang, and it was Donald asking if I'd come in to conduct his portion of the show, a job that I was happy to do. The house bandleader was Les Brown, whose regular band I'd always admired, and had hoped to be a part of someday.

At the first run-through I met Harbach, Vanoff, Brown and most of the staff. Everything seemed chaotic, but I was later to learn that's the nature of doing a massive show every week in the TV industry. The run-through is the first shot the production staff has at seeing how the material would be performed. The director gets an idea of how he wishes to videotape it, the scenic and lighting directors get their cues in mind, and the script supervisor gets a copy of the lyrics and dialogue. This all took place at the theatre on a Wednesday afternoon.

Thursday was camera-blocking day; a long and tiresome day beginning at eight o'clock in the morning. It's a day of stop-and-start cues for the rehearsal pianist, (me) so the cameramen could set their shots and the remainder of the staff could familiarize themselves with the pacing of the production. After a dinner break, the orchestra arrived for a pre-recording session and rehearsal beginning at seven o'clock in the evening. For Donald's portion I was at the piano, as both conductor and accompanist. Friday morning was a camera run-thru again with just piano. That was followed by an afternoon dress rehearsal with the full thirty-piece orchestra, and then an evening show. Both dress and show were videotaped with an audience, mainly as a protective backup in case something went awry during the performance. Very often when a mistake would occur, the video editor would edit out the error, and insert the same segment of the dress rehearsal in its place. The shots of the audience laughing or applauding were edited in to the cuts in order to make the edits less obvious to the home viewer.

Although I wasn't privy to the actual happening, the pianist who had been hired for the show was told that day he had to do all the rehearsals as well as the show. Being a busy established studio musician he objected, since it would cut into his numerous record dates and other shows that he had scheduled. He handed in his notice at that time. John Fresco, the music contractor at ABC-TV, told me that Les Brown liked my work, and asked if I'd like to be the regular pianist. Needless to say I happily accepted, and I regretfully told Donald that I had to give him my two-week notice. He understood, and wished me the best. Our paths would often cross as the years went by, and we remain the best of acquaintances.

Through the years, young musicians have often asked me, how should they proceed to get a job in the studios. If I have any one thing to give in the way of advice, it's simply, "Try to be in the right place at the right time." So much of the music business is luck, but if it happens, you'd better have the experience and talent to back it up. Every job I did added another layer of experience to my realm of musical knowledge.

I could never learn these things in music school. Schools may teach basics and some advanced theoretical knowledge, but the actual work experience is where ninety percent of the necessary skills are learned. The Catskills...the saloons...the strip joints. All these diverse situations had given me the wherewithal to feel confident that I could play whatever was put in front of me.

My association with Les Brown was to last many years even though at the end of the first season of the Hollywood Palace, he was replaced by Mitchell Ayers, long-time conductor for Perry Como. Mitch cast an imposing shadow and had been nicknamed "Godzilla" by the band on the Como show in New York. I later learned he had risen from a fiddle player in a pit orchestra to assistant conductor, then to full fledged conductor. His knowledge of the inner workings of harmony and theory were nil, but he had a great knack of instilling confidence in the various artists. It didn't take me long to pick up on this, so I stopped asking him questions about wrong notes. If I did he'd lower his glasses, glare at me and tell me that I should know how to fix the mistake. As a conductor, he was good for singers, sensing a musical cadence and floating right across the top of it. This allowed the vocalist freedom in phrasing and room for variances. As for understanding arrangements, he didn't do well at reading a score, so he insisted on having piano/conductor parts made. These are essentially condensed scores playable on piano with lyrics written boldly throughout. I would use them for rehearsals, marking the changes as I went along. At the first orchestra rehearsal, he ascended the podium with the utmost confidence and an air of total control. Initially, I thought of a great way to mark the parts: Color code them, and thereby make them obvious at a glance. Red for "ritard," yellow for an upcoming tempo change, green for "accelerando," and so on. What I didn't know was that Mitch was colorblind and at the rehearsal, all he saw were gray splotches at various locations on the music. Another good idea shot to hell!

During one of our initial contacts, Mitch took me aside, and confessed that he didn't know a lot of answers. That was to be my job. I'd be paid well over scale if in fact I'd whisper the answer to any musical question that may have come down from the strings, or brass or woodwinds. If there was a note in doubt within the orchestra, he'd look at me and I'd mumble something like,

"It's a D flat."

Mitch would then look at his part, and loudly proclaim,

"It's a D flat!"

His main concern was that I never show up his weaknesses in the presence of the orchestra. I later learned that he had a similar arrangement with New York pianist Billy Roland during the Perry Como series. Mitch and I got along well, and this led to even more TV work.

As music contractor for ABC-TV in Hollywood, John Fresco's job was to hire the musicians. I was on his "A-list" for keyboardists and before long, I was doing TV shows almost every day of the week. At one point, I was doing "Hollywood Palace," "The King Family Hour," "The Tom Jones Show" and "The Milton Berle Comedy Hour." These were weekly shows, so I was kept busy running from one theatre to another. In addition, there were also telethons, so my life was a world of music.

"The Tom Jones Show" which showcased the top pop star from Wales was taped partially in London and the rest of the year in Los Angeles. The availability of American musical stars was the primary reason for bringing the show stateside, and it allowed me to be in the position of pianist and utility arranger. The musical director was Johnny Spence, a ruddy-faced good-natured Brit who was a very talented arranger. Along with him also came guitarist "Big Jim" Sullivan and drummer Ronnie Verrell. This group was extremely talented and had a great capacity for partying, as they could consume enormous amounts of alcoholic beverages at any time of the day or night and still perform unerringly. My association with Spence allowed me to visit London after the taping season had ended, where I was introduced to many of England's finer musicians.

One anecdote from London concerns the late Phil Seaman,

drummer and percussionist well known around the British music scene, not only for his innate talent but also for his heavy use of narcotics. Word has it that Seaman, while in the pit orchestra in a London stage production of "The King and I", had nodded off during the performance. As will often happen, he snapped out of his narcotic-induced stupor with a start, thinking he'd missed a cue. He grabbed a large mallet and proceeded to whack a tam-tam, a large oriental gong. As it turned out, the cue hadn't yet occurred, and there was soft, romantic dialogue being spoken onstage. As the silence was shattered by the vibrations echoing from the gong, the actors peered into the pit glaring at Phil. Realizing that this was a major goof, Seaman stood up, faced the audience, and loudly proclaimed, "Dinner is served!" With that, he slumped back to his drum throne and immediately went back to sleep. True story!

Joe Lipman had been brought out from New York by Vanoff & Harbach as chief arranger for "The Hollywood Palace." He had also been an arranger on most of their previous variety shows. A former pianist with Jimmy Dorsey, Joe had the reputation of being one of the fastest arrangers in the industry. Even with speed as an asset, he eventually became overwhelmed since he had only a day and a half to orchestrate the music for an entire one-hour show. We had a dozen dancers every week, and the choreographer made up new routines for each show in which I was rehearsal pianist. Joe knew I was also an arranger, so he allocated the dance production numbers to my pencil. I was given an office next to his at the theatre, and we'd be in contact continually as we'd often sit up until three o'clock in the morning finishing scores for the show later that day. The bleary-eyed copyists would be nearby to take what we had written and extract the various parts to put on the instrumentalists' music stands. This was not an easy job, but being a young man I had the stamina to handle the workload. It also helped boost my income level, since arrangers were paid a scale far above the average instrumentalist. It was all the years of writing, plus the union pension contributions that would allow an early retirement.

For seven years The "Hollywood Palace" was a Saturday night fixture, airing immediately after the Lawrence Welk Hour on ABC-TV. Initially, we did thirty-nine shows per season with thirteen reruns. This allowed me to take off the entire summer and through our union, we would be repaid seventy-five percent of our initial earnings every time a show re-ran. A sweet deal, one might say!

I would spend the summers hanging around in Las Vegas with old friends and doing other freelance jobs either in Los Angeles or Las Vegas. One summer I got a call to play atop the Dunes Hotel in Las Vegas for tea and cocktail hour with a young female violinist. We played light classics and show tunes from 4 to 7 PM. Our dressing room was a regular hotel room, and during the breaks we'd retreat there and watch TV while stretched out on the bed. It didn't take long to figure that we could do something more interesting on the bed than watch the local news, so we began necking during intermissions. We managed to keep our hormones under control throughout the engagement. That job ended as the next "Hollywood Palace" season was about to begin. That meant I had to return to Los Angeles.

For two summers, I toured with the Les Brown Band of Renown. To keep myself occupied on the seemingly endless bus trips, I'd do a new arrangement for the band each week. This kept the boredom to a minimum and also boosted the income level. It was a dream realized, to be a member of Les' great sounding aggregation. The band would usually tour during the summer months when television shows were on hiatus. In September Les would once again begin the Dean Martin Show and the Bob Hope series over at NBC.

The "Hollywood Palace" began in 1964 and continued on through 1970. In those seven years I had the opportunity to play, and in some cases arrange, for practically every entertainment luminary that was around in that era. Frequent guests for whom I wrote arrangements were Bing Crosby, Sammy Davis Jr., Milton Berle, Tony Randall, Frank Sinatra and Judy Garland to name a few. The host of long-standing comedians included Jack

E. Leonard, Gene Baylos, Dick Shawn, Shecky Greene and Joey Bishop among others. The producers also had a deal in place with a European circus, which annually would tour the United States. They would cordon off the parking lot on Vine Street adjacent to the theatre, and for about a week would videotape high-wire acts, elephants, dog acts, monkey acts and even tigers in a cage. They would insert these segments into the ensuing shows at which time the orchestra would add music. Regardless of how many edits and cuts there were in a chunk of videotape, the music had to provide the continuity. That's why it was done in postproduction.

In order to achieve some semblance of audience reaction and participation, they would often bring the animal acts indoors and have the performance take place on the stage. The cameras would shoot from the rear of the theatre, showing the silhouette of the audience in the camera's foreground. The audience, however, at these times was comprised of soft-bodied mannequins with various hats and wigs atop their heads. The liability insurance didn't cover the possibility of a tiger breaking loose and mauling a theatre patron. Once we were doing a wild animal performance when a tiger did get loose. It took all the wiles of the trainer to run through the dummies in the theatre cracking his whip, and eventually getting the big cat back into its cage.

We had one stagehand, Ed Holland, who didn't like animals. The animals sensed it, and every time one had an opportunity to misbehave, Ed was the recipient. Whenever he passed close to the backside of Bertha the elephant she would loudly break wind, precisely when Ed was at the closest and most vulnerable point. A tiger once urinated all over Ed. I once had a photo that I'd hung up in the music office at the Palace showing Ed shoveling up elephant droppings the size of steaming basketballs, while Bing Crosby was looking on. Whenever this sort of occurrence happened, especially if we had a live audience nearby, producer Bill Harbach would signal to me to play something, preferably jazz while the wranglers and stagehands shoveled and mopped up the residual mess. In our rhythm section was the famous guitarist Barney Kessel who had a truly wonderful Oklahoma-bred down-home wit. Years later while attending a jazz concert on Hilton Head Island I reunited backstage with Barney and asked him how the jazz scene was going, to which he answered,

"Not too great. I can't seem to get inspired unless there's an elephant nearby."

The soft-bodied dummies would get tossed in a heap in the theatre basement when they weren't being used. It created an almost surreal sight made even funnier when our first trombonist Milt Bernhardt would squoosh in the midst of them, with a blank stare and remain motionless while people walked by. Someone took a photo of that which also hung on the wall of the music office. I don't know what became of these priceless photos once the show closed.

One of the saddest days during the run of the show was when the news came that Mitch Ayres had been killed by a hit-and-run driver while in Las Vegas. I'm not a sentimental sort when I hear of people passing, and whatever emotions I have are usually kept in check. This time I cried all night when I thought of the bond that I had established with Mitch. With all his faults, he was a mentor in so many ways. I learned a lot about the actual art of conducting while serving under his baton that was usually a pencil, which he would snap in half upon getting frustrated. I'll never forget his remark when songstress Kate Smith was verbally abusive to him and the orchestra. He snapped a pencil in half, looked at me and muttered,

"I'd like to slit her corset and watch her spread to death!"

Probably the simplest choice for a replacement for Mitch would have been me, since I knew the show inside out. However, in Hollywood, one was always pigeonholed. In the eyes of the producers I was strictly a pianist, even though on many occasions I would conduct when Mitch was occupied with some other project. This wouldn't become an issue, since the show only had one more season in which to run.

Nick Vanoff and Bill Harbach brought out a conductor from New York who happened to be a long time friend of mine going back to the Lester Lanin days. Nick Perito had taken over as conductor for Perry Como when Mitch moved to Hollywood and now had once again succeeded him. Nick is a tremendously talented arranger, conductor and pianist, and through the ensuing years, we worked in tandem. We arranged so similarly that nobody could tell where he left off and I picked up. He was also the arranger-conductor for Steve Lawrence and Eydie Gorme at that time and provided my first introduction to them. Nick took the helm of the "Hollywood Palace" for the last year of its production.

The final week of the "Hollywood Palace" was truly a sad one. The staff and crew had been there from the onset, and it was truly one big happy family. The producers tossed a party, and the curtain rang down for the last time on our seven-year series. In subsequent years we would all find ourselves working with the same production family on other shows in ensuing television seasons.

HOLLYWOOD PALACE, 1966,
WITH COMEDIAN GENE BAYLOS

CHAPTER 13

THE "HEE-HAW" DAYS

The 1960s saw a plethora of musical variety shows on television. Because of them I was able to earn a comfortable living doing something that I loved: making music. There were all kinds of television fare, good and bad. Some shows were less than thrilling, but each and every project had a flavor unto itself and proved to be a learning experience.

One show I worked on that doesn't appear on my resume was a summer replacement variety series in 1969. It was a bit of corny fluff that had little or no future, or so thought CBS and the producers. Former "Hollywood Palace" producer Nick Vanoff had partnered with comedy writers Frank Peppiatt and John Aylesworth in a new company, Yongestreet Productions. They had come up with this idea and successfully pitched it to CBS. The show with the dubious title of "Hee-Haw" was to be taped in Nashville. It was a country bumpkin spoof that was simply a slot-filler for CBS. At that time nearly all the country stars lived and worked in that vicinity. The production company asked if I'd go down to be in charge of the music, and once again I accepted.

Upon arrival at the Nashville airport I was met by Associate Producer Al Simon, also formerly of the Hollywood Palace staff, who drove me to a Holiday Inn on James Robertson Parkway. As I proceeded to register, the lady behind the front desk asked in a Tennessee twang,

"Do you want the trucks or the trains?"

"Beg pardon?"

"Trucks or trains?" she reiterated.

As I was to find out, the hotel was sandwiched between a main highway and a railroad track. I had a choice of what I wanted to keep me awake. I opted for the trains.

Being tired from traveling, I ordered a steak dinner from room service, finished it and put the tray outside my room. I managed to sleep through the night despite the occasional rumbling of a long freight train outside my window. The following morning, I got dressed ready to take on the television task that lay ahead. As I exited my room I noticed my dinner tray was still outside the door, and there was a sizeable rat having morning breakfast on my leftovers. Welcome to Nashville.

The first item when I reached the "Hee-Haw" production office was to get transferred to another hotel. There was a Ramada Inn nearby, so I decided to take my chances there. I had one of the station's gofers move my luggage and do a check-in at the Ramada while I went in to meet the local musicians. I introduced myself to the players amid some rather dubious glances and heard rumblings of "Hollywood hotshot" from a couple of them. They didn't appear too friendly, and as I reached in my attaché case for some music I'd composed for a theme, one of them drawled,

"We don't read that kinda stuff down here."

"Oh? What kinda stuff do you read down here?" I asked.

It didn't take me long to find out that standard music notation was unknown and unpracticed by the Nashvillians. They each had a steno pad, and a system of *solfeggio* using numerals. This way, they could play in any key simply by indicating a I, IV or V chord. The *capo* on the stringed instruments could be placed in different positions on the neck of the instruments, thereby putting them in different keys. Regardless of which key the song may be written, the fingerings would be the same. A few violin players could read, but the rhythm players frowned on such learning. The busiest studio piano player in town was blind, if that can give any indication of how differently things were done.

Production began on "Hee-Haw", and I quickly became accustomed to the ways of the local players. Eventually they lost their defensive hostility to the "Hollywood hotshot." They had developed their own system, and it worked quite well, I must say. I couldn't function as an arranger in the normal sense, but if I played what I wanted on the piano, they'd scribble their markings on the steno pad and somehow pull it off better than if I'd written it out note for note for them.

(See figures 1 & 2)

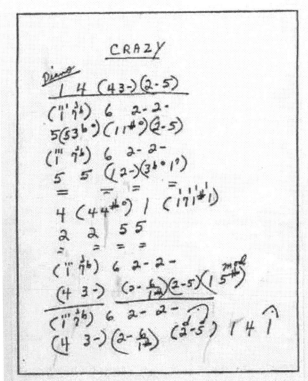

Jimmy Capps — Lead guitarist for the Grand Ole Opry staff band since 1968. Jimmy writes many of the charts that are used on the Opry.

Figure 1

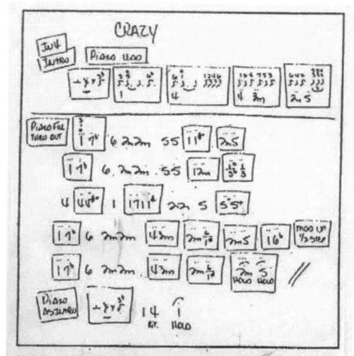

Lura Foster — "...writes the best charts in town," said Jerry Whitehurst, the music director for the "Nashville Now" show. Lura has written all the charts for the "Nashville Now" band since the show began five years ago. Lura's charts look extra complicated, but they include instructions for the entire rhythm section, strings and horns.

Figure 2

As the weeks progressed, a parade of luxury busses would pull in behind the studio facility and out would come well-traveled, bedraggled and often hung-over country music stars. It was a culture quite foreign to me but seemingly very normal to the local staff. Tammy Wynette would be bruised and battered from one of then-husband George Jones' drinking and punching bouts. The makeup department would be pressed into overtime trying to hide her lumps and bruises, while the lighting director made sure the shadows hid anything that was obvious beyond repair. Jones would practically have to be propped up to sing his numbers and with a glassy-eyed stare and unblinking, would somehow twang his way through his vocal solos. As soon as we'd call a wrap, they'd be back on the bus with their band members and off to the next bout of drinking and fighting.

The regulars were Buck Owens and his Buckaroos, Roy Clark, Grandpa Jones and Junior Samples. Junior wasn't much different in real life than the morbidly obese bumpkin that he portrayed on the show. Buck tended to be a bit surly while Roy was a hard-playing, hard-drinking but cheerful guitar-picker. One morning, while trying to rid himself of a hangover, Roy ingested an entire bottle of Tabasco sauce. As a result he ended up in the emergency room of a local hospital. This seemed especially unfortunate since Roy was truly an excellent guitarist, especially in the country and bluegrass genre.

When our videotaping days would wrap up, we'd all go back to the Ramada and have some chow, ending up afterwards in the bar. I was single at the time, and was always scouting. At the time, most of the girls I encountered in Nashville somehow appeared to have Rickets, Scurvy or Beriberi. They didn't look healthy, and I could only assume some sort of vitamin deficiency. The barmaid at our hotel was a gal named Mickey, who wore tights and fishnet stockings. Her hairdo was typical of Nashville back then, piled high and lacquered into stone. Her fingernails were bitten down to the quick, and her cuticles looked as if she'd been working on the underside of a '47 Chevy. Al Simon and I would sit there night after night hoping that if we drank enough, sooner or later she might look good to one of us. The weeks went by. She never did achieve the necessary aura.

I was quite relieved when our final shooting day ended, and I headed directly to the airport to board my flight to Los Angeles. When I was asked how I spent my summer, I'd answer,

"In misery."

Surprisingly, "Hee-Haw" turned out to be a national

success, and CBS decided to renew it for the following season. By then I'd forgotten the weeks spent in a land that had a culture and a dialect I couldn't fathom. I once again agreed to go back for another batch of summer replacements. The show became so popular that it actually topped the Nielsen ratings. It was so successful they decided to make a regular full season show of it, rather that just a summer replacement. I guess nobody ever went broke underestimating the taste of the American public. It was then that I said to the producer,

"Take me out, Coach. They can do it just as well without me."

They did. Pianist Jerry Whitehurst took over as music maven for the run of the show, which stretched over many years. It ran up until the President of CBS decided that it was too rural for his Park Avenue taste, so he cancelled it as well as "Green Acres" and any other hit television shows that had a twinge of bumpkin-ism attached to them. His aim was to take CBS on the high road, but his plan backfired and took CBS down into the cellar of the three major networks. "Hee-Haw" resurfaced in syndication on independent channels for over 20 years. Great! Just as long as I wasn't in Nashville, more power to it.

So far, I can't say that the omission of "Hee-Haw" on my resume has harmed my musical career in any way. Although I've not returned to the Nashville area since that time, I understand it's come a long way since the '60s and has a thriving country music industry. There is also a broader-based music scene that incorporates some fine jazz musicians, an excellent symphony plus other classical and commercial ensembles. I'd probably enjoy it at today's level. Hopefully, I'd be able to avoid the trucks or the trains.

CHAPTER 14

THE NBC YEARS

The turbulent decade of the '70s had begun. In a very frightening way, the Watts riots had come and gone, and I had seen a good portion of Los Angeles go up in smoke from my apartment balcony. My mother and stepfather, still living in Boca Raton, continued their alcoholic binges. The two of them had a pattern known as *enabling*, a very destructive psychological game that was played out on a subconscious level. One would be drinking heavily while the other provided the means or excuses for the behavior. My only feeling of relief regarding this new relationship was that it would get her off my back with her late-night, drunken telephone tirades about what a selfish, thoughtless person I was. I'm sure she felt I neglected her, but the truth was she became a very evil person when under the influence of alcohol, which by the way, was most all the time. I tried to keep my distance and occasionally would call her out of duty and a modicum of respect. Now Joe would be the target for her tantrums, and that allowed me to breathe a sigh of relief.

Color TV had begun in the latter half of the '60s, and the television medium had taken on a new allure for the viewing public. Variety programs were plentiful. There were shows such as Ed Sullivan, Carol Burnett, Dean Martin, Bob Hope, Tom Jones, Lawrence Welk, Don Knotts, Phyllis Diller, Glenn Campbell, Sonny and Cher and others too numerous to mention. Much of my life had been immersed in those productions along with some sitcoms, for which I was called upon to supply music. My reputation had grown throughout Hollywood. Recording sessions and commercial jingles abounded. I was never in need of work, since the mindset of the nabobs in tinseltown was, "If he's good enough to do all those network shows then he must be good enough for us. Get him." This is all a part of the Hollywood ladder. All studio musicians go through the five-stage process, as I had mentioned earlier. It happens thusly:

1) "Who's Bob Alberti?
2) "Get me Bob Alberti!"
3) "Get me someone who sounds like Bob Alberti!"
4) "Get me a young Bob Alberti!"
5) "Who's Bob Alberti?"

As the musical trends changed (and those changes came rapidly), I was on top of the heap, only to find a year or so later, my place had been usurped by someone with longer hair and love beads. A situation comes to mind that occurred with a radio and TV commercial company, otherwise known as a "jingle factory." When I first started working for them, the bigwigs in the upper offices were the typical Madison Avenue three-button-suit types. I was secure and comfortable in knowing that I was first-call pianist on all of their sessions. Somewhere in the mid to late '60s, I noticed that the executives were mimicking the mode of dress and hairstyles of the free-love generation. Needless to say they looked a bit silly since most of them were middle-aged men who had barely any fringe left of what may have been a hairline in earlier days. However, as was the case with Hollywood then, and still is today, trendiness is overwhelming, and if a person is not a stalwart who is secure in his own image, it's easy to be swept up into the latest craze.

Since I liked my image, I was not about to change. No beard, no long sideburns, no bell-bottom slacks. I couldn't help but notice that there were fewer calls as the months went on from this particular agency. As it boiled down to zero I confronted one of the executives. His answer was that I no longer fit the youthful image that they were trying to convey to their clients, and I played too well!

Played too well? That was a switch! At the time piano-pounders such as Carole King were all the rage. They felt that my touch was too professional, and I really wasn't in tune with the L.S.D. generation. I'm grateful for small favors, and this was one of them!

This was also the generation of Woodstock, the VW buses and the flower children. It was the free love era. I recall lamenting as I looked at the youth of the day with their psychedelic vans with queen-size mattresses in the back, how I had a turndown from a young lady many years earlier because I owned a Nash. The Nash was renown for the ability to convert the back seat into a bed, and apparently this girl's mother had learned of that convenience. I was on the "do not date" list in Brooklyn. If I had only been born ten years later(Sigh).

The era was not totally barren for my surging hormones. I had my share of relationships with comely flight attendants, Hollywood wannabees, and other nubile lasses whose paths intersected mine. I made my share of mistakes, and the best way I can currently rationalize them is to consider them learning experiences. One major lapse in judgment happened in 1965.

I had gone to a club in the San Fernando Valley, a suburban bedroom community northwest of Los Angeles where a group of my friends were appearing. Stan Worth was a singer-entertainer-pianist who held forth at local nightspots with his trio. His bassist Mort Klanfer was a long time friend and the drummer was Allen Goodman, who I had known since my early days in Brooklyn. The club was the *Ruddy Duck* in Studio City, and I was comfortably perched at the piano bar. A rather attractive young lady to my left tapped me on the shoulder and pointed to the left cuff of my shirt, where I had my initials embroidered.

"Excuse me," she said, "Isn't that an odd place for a laundry mark?"

I rapidly filtered the remark through my gray matter and decided that was her ploy at being humorous. It was my introduction to Anita.

The following year I still couldn't decide whether that

remark was humor or naiveté. There had been a few more along the way, and another one that comes to mind was when I ordered Steak Tartare at a Sunset Strip boite. It was mixed together tableside, beautifully formed and presented raw, as it should be. When the platter was placed in front of me, she looked quizzically at the maitre'd and asked,

"Aren't you gonna cook it?"

Anita was a vivacious and lively sort, always good for a laugh and a good time. She was relatively young, divorced and the mother of three-year-old fraternal twins. Her nature was that of being a defender of the underdog. It was a time when demonstrations were the pastime of discontented and seemingly disenfranchised young people. I was conservative on some issues, liberal on others, but generally a middle-of-the-road path seemed most comfortable. Anita was definitely a full-blown liberal and, as far as I know, may still be to this day. There was rarely a protest of one sort or another that she missed attending, and it seemed to me that she had a knee-jerk reaction to any demonstration to help (or hinder) an oppressed group, depending on one's viewpoint. She became friendly with Beverlee Goodman, the former wife of Allen Goodman in an alliance whereby both women were supportive in the sign-carrying brigade. I distanced myself from these activities as much as possible. Anita was also flirtatious. I would say that she was the female incarnation of Will Rogers. She never met a man she didn't like.

I don't know what I was thinking since I never had any desire to end up with a couple of kids in my household, especially, someone else's kids. In my time spent with Anita, I tried to always come by after the youngsters had gone to bed so I wouldn't have to deal with the shenanigans of two ever-battling three year olds. I deluded myself to where they didn't exist in my mind. If I had to define my own personal Hell, it would be going to heaven and being put in charge of the day-care center. I could never relate to young children and always got extremely tense when faced with any interaction them. Anyway, our relationship grew into about an eight-month marriage that came to an abrupt end when I realized I really didn't like the thought of being a lifelong stepfather. I would come home from work, pour a water tumbler full of vodka and after about fifteen minutes, I couldn't care if the kids destroyed each other. My escape was drinking, or sitting holed up in one room of our apartment that was designated as my office. Nobody dare enter that sanctuary while I was doing my orchestral scoring. Life took on a morose aura as I realized that I'd made a terrible mistake. I approached Anita with the thought of an annulment, and although it was not what she wanted, she realized that I was not good for her offspring and probably would remain that way as long as we were together. We agreed to the annulment.

Upon parting, I embarked on the good life of the esteemed bachelor. After all, Hugh Hefner had made a fortune from that path in life, so if it was there for the taking, perhaps I might get a bit of the backwash. As a post script to my relationship with Anita, I later found out that in 1996 she ran for congress in Palm Springs, California, against Republican Sonny Bono (of "Sonny & Cher" fame.) She ran as a liberal Democrat but lost, due to the heavily conservative Palm Springs population. I must give her full credit as a single mother and for her determination to succeed in a hostile world. My dating continued into the '70s. I had a comfortable bachelor pad and a little black book with enough names to keep me happy.

During this time I'd met and worked with comedienne Phyllis Diller when she had a show at NBC. Phyllis is a truly grand lady, one of my favorite people, and a consummate musician. Most people are unaware that Phyllis was classically trained as a pianist. She also played harpsichord and on rare occasion, soprano saxophone, (even before *Kenny G* popularized it)! After her weekly TV series had concluded, Phyllis decided to go on tour doing her piano act as a fund-raiser for symphonies around the country. She enlisted my aid to help her learn Beethoven's First Piano Concerto in C minor. She had two pianos in her home, facing one another. She would play the solo part and I would do the orchestral portion from a reduced score to familiarize her with the musical entrances. I toured with her as she played various cities throughout the United States and Canada. On our first stop in Vancouver, B.C., we checked into our respective rooms:

On stage with Phyllis Diller, Summer 1972

A surprise visitor on Hilton Head Island, May 1997.

Phyllis, her road secretary and myself. As I was relaxing on the bed watching TV, I heard a knock on the door. I got up and opened it only to find an empty hallway. I reclined once again on the bed when the knock occurred once more. Again I opened the door to the hallway to find nothing. The knock continued, and I finally realized it had come from the adjoining room. I opened my side of the connecting door and in the doorway stood the road secretary in a see-through negligee. I was invited next door for a nightcap, and I'll leave the rest to your imagination.

A few months went by, and the road secretary found a more suitable job opportunity in television and handed in her notice to Phyllis. She was replaced with a cute little red-haired girl from Santa Barbara. It didn't take too long before the fires lit between us and the road was as much fun as always. In time when this lady left for greener pastures, Phyllis was interviewing applicants for the job. She forewarned them, "Watch out for my musical director. He wore out my last two secretaries!" That was followed by Phyllis' hysterical laugh, her well-known trademark.

I didn't have a lot of free time in between jobs during this thriving musical period. In my spare moments, I'd frequent *The Ruddy Duck* fantasizing about possible TV shows I would love to produce. I always wanted to do a spoof of "Medic," the hospital show of the 60s, with Howdy-Doody as a guest star, in which he'd be circumcised with a pencil sharpener. Another was a crime-based show where the Pillsbury Doughboy would be found guilty of viewer-annoyance, and would be executed by being placed in a microwave oven on *high* for fifteen minutes. None of those ever came to fruition, but I could always have some fun dreaming up these absurdities while sipping a good single-malt scotch at the bar.

Back on the Hollywood scene, after the demise of the Hollywood Palace, Les Brown spoke with me. At the time Les was at NBC as musical director of the Bob Hope series as well as the Dean Martin show. He asked if I would be an arranger on both shows, augmenting the work being done by arrangers Jay

Hill on the Hope series and Van Alexander on the Martin shows. It sounded like a good offer so I gladly accepted. The music contractor at NBC was Al Lapin, a diminutive man who was always dressed to the nines. Al had become extremely wealthy a few years earlier along with his two sons when they founded the original International House of Pancakes. When NBC had been built in a rather desolate area in Burbank, California, in the early '50s there were no reasonably decent restaurants near the studios. NBC had no commissary at that time, so the only place to eat lunch was at a "roach-coach" operated by a chap named Ben. "Ben's Truck" was it for NBC. Breakfast, lunch and dinner. Ben knew all, heard all and saw all. He knew your show was cancelled long before you did, and usually the performers learned their fate from Ben's gossiping.

Al Lapin and sons decided to open their eating establishment within a couple of blocks of the studio complex. The ensuing success of the business led to the I.H.O.P. franchising operation that is still going today. Al and his family literally made millions. However, his love of music was so great that he kept his job as NBC music contractor until many years later when old age and dementia took its toll.

Al hadn't taken too much notice of my presence until I was playing piano for Danny Kaye in Las Vegas. Danny's long-time pianist Sammy Prager had suddenly been hospitalized with a detached retina and could not travel. I was asked to be a last-minute replacement for Sammy by Sid Kaye, (no relation to Danny,) who was Danny's drummer/conductor and a neighbor of mine. Danny was known to be very difficult to work for, but to help Sid in this emergency, I accepted.

Sammy had been Danny's only pianist for over twenty years, and for me to walk into a position that has been held that long was an immediate trap. The familiarity with Danny's every move was second nature to Sammy but completely new to me. To make matters worse, when Sid went to show me the piano book, it was empty. Sammy had memorized everything, then destroyed the parts in an effort to make his position secure. I had four days to learn the show, which I did by walking around with a portable cassette player and a recording of a previous show they had recorded a month earlier.

Al Lapin came to see the show since he knew Danny quite well and was prominently seated ringside. After the show a note was delivered to me in my dressing room with Al Lapin's business card attached, telling me to call him when I returned to Los Angeles. He was impressed with what he heard and upon calling him the following week, he told me that Jimmy Rowles who had been the staff pianist at NBC was leaving and the position was open. Would I be interested? It didn't take but seconds to answer in the affirmative and let him know that I'd be happy to be on board.

At that particular time, NBC was the busiest network in the area of variety. In addition to all the weekly one-hour shows that utilized live orchestras, they also had Johnny Carson's Tonight Show that had moved out to Burbank from New York. That show aired five nights per week and had a sixteen-piece orchestra, a collection of the greatest jazz and studio players ever assembled in Los Angeles. I was fortunate to have been the alternate pianist on the show from about 1974 to 1983. Doc Severinsen would very often travel to do personal appearances, during which time he'd take the key rhythm section players on tour with him, necessitating the alternates to move in. Tommy Newsom would take over the band in Doc's absence, and besides yours truly at the piano, I had the pleasure of such great associates as Louie Bellson or Colin Bailey at the drums, guitarists Peter Woodford and Bob Bain and bassist Don Baldini. Every position in the orchestra had to have two alternates who would be approved by both Doc and Tommy. I was one who would cover in the absence of Ross Tompkins, the first-string pianist. Ross' nickname was "The Phantom," who in addition to traveling with Doc, would on occasion call in at about two o'clock in the afternoon, and inform Al Lapin that he was at his family home in Florida and had missed his connecting flight back to Burbank. I would either be in the NBC building, or at home, only about ten minutes away. I'd get the panic call to get over to the studio, dressed and ready for a 3:15 rehearsal and a 5:30 videotaping.

I recall one Tonight Show when I was at the piano, Ed McMahon and Johnny Carson were into a humorous discussion concerning the pronunciation of the word *pianist*. Carson said it was pronounced *pi-an-ist,* while McMahon contended that the accent should be on the second syllable, *Pi-an-ist.* They decided to settle the matter by asking someone who should know, and before I knew what was happening, the camera was on me. The question was posed,

"Is it pi-an-ist or pi-an-ist?" and my instinctive answer was, "It's piano player!"

That was followed by a guffaw from the band and the audience, accompanied by a blank stare from Carson and McMahon. I don't recall ever being asked another question while on the air.

Al Lapin was a delightful man, who gained his education on the streets of the lower east side of Manhattan. He had no formal education, and tended to misuse words at every possible turn. His malapropisms are legendary, and in fact Gil Falco, the lead trombonist with the band wrote them down in a much-prized collection, and titled it, WHAT THE AL-LAPINED? An example of Al's conversation took place when trumpeter Al Vizzuti went out on tour with jazz pianist Chick Corea. Someone asked Lapin why they hadn't seen Vizutti on the band recently. Al's reply was,

"He's been out on a date with some chick from Korea."

I once asked Al Lapin about the pitfalls of operating a restaurant. He pinpointed the three biggest problems:

"Spillage, spoilage and stealage."

A few more Lapin-isms:

"This situation is abdominal."

"There's another Masonic boom." (Jet noise.)

"That's all water over the bridge."

"The union's doing an admiral job."

"This is a real dilemon."

"I flew to New York on a TWA Consolation."

"A bird in the hand is worth two around the corner."

"I knew Tommy Dorsey when he played trombone."

"On TV last night, I saw Norman's Clabernacle Choir," (Mormon Tabernacle Choir.)

I could go on and on about how Al came across with his pearls of wisdom. He was generous to a fault, and if he liked a particular musician he'd make sure that player ended up doing every show that came through NBC.

I was one of the fortunate ones.

CHAPTER 15

NAME THAT TUNE, BOB HOPE AND MORE

The music industry in the 1970s was alive and healthy. Telethons had sprung up for every imaginable cause, and year after year I managed to do my share of them. The Variety Club, Cerebral Palsy, flood victim relief, you name it, I've done it. So called "specials," (i.e. non-series) abounded, and as an arranger I had the opportunity to write charts for many of them. Some of the shows included stars such as Suzanne Somers, Dorothy Hamill, Olivia Newton-John, Ben Vereen, Mary Tyler Moore, Neil Sedaka, Rona Barrett, Perry Como, Tony Orlando and Shari Lewis. The special with Miss Lewis led to a series of 26 shows in 1975-1976, called "The Shari Show." Her material was clever and well executed, but the subject matter pertained primarily to children, and my musical interest was definitely in another direction.

Then there were the sitcoms, and although I didn't care for most of them, by today's standards they were gems. I was lucky enough to be hired to write and perform music for shows such as "Maude," starring Bea Arthur, "Sanford and Son," with Redd Foxx, and "C.P.O. Sharkey" with Don Rickles. There was also a short-lived gothic-horror sitcom on N.B.C. called "Highcliffe Manor," a season of "Hizzonner" starring David Huddleston plus a plethora of pilot shows that never made the schedule.

While all this was happening, I had a call from Ralph Edwards of "Truth or Consequences" and "This is Your Life" fame. At a meeting in his Hollywood office, he informed me that he was about to revive a TV musical game show that was popular in the early '50s, called "Name That Tune." He asked if I'd be interested in helping formulate the show and lead the orchestra for the pilot. This sounded like it was right up my alley, so I accepted the project.

The production staff involved with the show included Harry Salter, a diminutive older man who one would never guess had anything to do with the music business. Yet, he had been the brain trust and bandleader of the original series, and owned the copyright to the show title. He and Ralph Edwards were to be partners in the show's revival. Along with Harry came his librarian and musicologist, Harvey Bacal. Over the ensuing weeks and months, I tried to warm up to Harvey, but he was the epitome of the Yiddish word "noodge." He was always underfoot, whispering suggestions, most without merit, and tried to assert his importance at any and every opportunity. Harvey would eventually become the bane of my existence in months to follow. He would sidle up to the conductor's podium with a "suggestion" for every song we played, as to the proper tempo, or the intent of the composer, basically all irrelevant to the type of show we were doing. Eventually, I shoved the baton in his hand, and said,

"Harvey, it's yours! You want to be the leader, be my guest!"

"No! No!" answered Harvey. "You're the leader!"

"Then give me the stick. There's only one motorman to a train. Just stay the hell out of my sight!"

That would get him off my back for a couple of shows, after which he'd begin to wheedle his way back to his original annoying position. This sort of confrontation was a fairly regular occurrence during the run of "Name That Tune."

The pilot was done with a twelve-piece band that consisted of three brass, three woodwinds, four rhythm, harp and percussion. The show had a limited budget, so I did the most with the least. I always felt that any last chord, if given a tympani roll and rolling harp glissando would sound as big as a house. It did, despite the small orchestra.

A syndication company picked up the pilot for a series. We were to tape one show a week for syndication to air on non-network stations around the country. We went into production at station KTLA, which at the time was owned by former cowboy singer-turned-millionaire Gene Autry. The studios were old and decrepit with rats feeding on the leftover donuts. However, the price for the studio rental was in the desired range, so that's where the nighttime shows were taped. Each show required a minimum of thirty-five arrangements of songs to be played for the contestants. Initially, I did all the arranging, and with the numbers not having to exceed thirty seconds in length, I managed easily to score the required number of songs.

Subsequently, in order to save on studio rental, the producers decided to tape three shows in a day, so the crew would be in for one long day rather than three shorter ones. That meant a hundred and five arrangements had to be written and copied for those show days. The stress started to show, since I was still doing the arranging on Bob Hope specials, some of the Dean Martin shows and occasionally playing on the "Tonight Show."

To add to the chaos, NBC decided that a morning version of "Name That Tune" to run five days a week would be in order. That delighted Ralph Edwards and Company but the workload increased for me. The band for the morning show was cut to five men (2 horns and three rhythm) and that made for easier writing. However, they would tape five shows in one day, which meant having one hundred seventy-five arrangements on the stand. We had one hour to rehearse all the charts for the day before the NBC Standards and Practices department would come and confiscate all the music. Due to a past history of fixing game shows, the legal department had to make sure that we had no contact with any of the contestants and went so far as to shuffling the order of the shows so that we wouldn't know which of the five shows was up until we got on the bandstand. They would pass out the music folder for the first show of the day, which may have been rehearsed fourth, second or at any point earlier in the day.

We'd tape two shows, break for lunch and come back to do three more. By the time we got to the fifth and final show of the day, we were one step away from being musically brain-dead. I'd open the music folder and see a song title, but would have no recall of ever having rehearsed that song. Sometimes I'd draw a blank on the tempo and the tune itself, so I'd throw a downbeat and miraculously the band would rescue me.

By this time I had enlisted three other talented arrangers, Bobby Hammack, Jay Hill and Joe Lipman to help grind out the pages for the required number of songs. It wasn't creative quality, but rather "music by the pound." I hired a bright young lady, DeeDee Daniel, who also worked at the musicians union, to count bars and type up the arranging bills to be submitted with the orchestra contracts. My every waking moment was spent either writing the arrangements or playing them. It felt as if I no longer knew where home was.

One big caveat went along with doing the music for this show. If we were to make a mistake in accuracy by playing anything other than the correct melody, causing the contestant lose the round, we could be challenged. If we were proven to be wrong the contestant would be awarded the fifty thousand dollar grand prize. This meant that we had to be flawless, and I can say that in the one hundred sixty-seven shows I did of "Name That Tune," never once did we make an error. Knowing the possible repercussions put added pressure on the members of the orchestra, but somehow, we managed to pull through with a perfect record.

Some of our production crew were less than friendly. One of the line producers had a hatred of facial hair. Beards, moustaches, any kind of hair growth would irk him no end. Although it was illegal, he would disqualify certain applicants for the show because they had some facial hair growth. We knew this, but it never got to the Standards and Practices people at the network. This chap was usually hostile and almost always insulting, even when paying someone a compliment. The time came for a surprise birthday party for him, which was my cue to go to a party store and buy bushy black beards for the rest of the office staff, including the women. As he entered the room, we all jumped out and yelled "Surprise!" It certainly was. He blanched, turning absolutely white, and I don't think he ever recovered for the remainder of the party. It eventually got back to him who the responsible individual was that spearheaded that prank, and I was informed a few weeks later that he decided to "make a change" in orchestras for the following season. By this time, I'd had more than enough of the show and was happy to get on with whatever else was happening in my life.

I had been dating a variety of young ladies throughout the early '70s, but as I approached the forty-year-old mark, the dating scene began to wear thin. During this stretch of work, I'd narrowed down my romantic endeavors to one lady, an attractive gal who I had met while working on a show titled "The Harlem Globetrotter's Popcorn Machine." At the time, I was casually seeing a Japanese exchange student, a bank teller, a divorcee and an airline flight attendant. The lady who really attracted me not only with her appearance but her innate intelligence and wit was Shirley Stein, an assistant to the producer of the Globetrotters show. As the production was underway, for some unknown reason the producer insisted that there be no after-hours fraternization among the staff. Shirley and I would circumvent this by meeting after hours at a club on Sunset Strip called "Sneaky Pete's," (how apropos) where a buddy of mine was playing piano. We established a meaningful relationship during our evening soirees, and saw more of each other as the days went on. One by one, I began dropping my other dating partners until it was down to just one: Shirley.

I asked Shirley if, when the production was finished, she'd be interested in joining me on a vacation in Hawaii. She gladly accepted, and before we knew it we were on board an airliner heading over to Kauai. This was all done very surreptitiously because of the *no socializing* edict that we'd been cleverly evading, or so we thought. We checked into our hotel, unpacked and decided to head downstairs for something frothy served in a coconut shell. As we opened the door to the hallway, the door immediately across the hall from us also swung open, and who

was there but the show producer? Shirley gave a silent gasp, said
"hi" and then nervously said,

"How's the weather been here?"

"How would I know?" he countered. "I was on the same
plane as you!"

Since our cover was blown, we decided to add an extra shot
of rum to our libation. As we sat at a patio table sipping the first
of many yet to come, I saw a large, hulking body at the bar. I
said to Shirley,

"If I didn't know better, I'd say that guy looks like Norm
Schwartz, our audio man."

It was…We'd just finished weeks of taping with him on the
Globetrotters, and here he was, also in Hawaii, same hotel. We
might as well have called a staff meeting. I quickly learned that
Hawaii was the spot for TV people to come and chill out after
putting a show to bed.

After a week of enjoyment and many Pu-Pu platters, we
returned home. I didn't know it at the time, but it would turn
out that she and I would eventually marry. That was well over
twenty-seven years ago, and I still am madly in love with her. I
wouldn't want it any other way.

During the '60s and '70s California had experienced an
unprecedented real estate boom. Home prices had skyrocketed,
and fortunately I'd had enough foresight to get in on the
upswing. I would buy a small house in a great neighborhood and
proceed to fix it up cosmetically. I'd then sell it a year later, take
the profits and invest in a slightly bigger and better house. I'd
worked my way up through about three or four properties when
I found a house in the suburb of Sherman Oaks. In 1973 I bought
the house for $42,000 and did some minor construction to add
a new master bedroom and bath. I was in it for a very short time
when Shirley moved in with me. We stayed together for about a
year and a half before we made the trip to a justice-of-the-peace
in Santa Monica to legitimize our relationship. I admit to being
gun-shy at the thought of marriage, since I was 40 years old and
had been a bachelor for a number of those years. Nonetheless,
I inherently sensed a good thing when I saw it, so I agreed to

get married. While waiting for the justice-of-the-peace to begin the ceremony, I was intently watching a Dodger baseball game on the television in his parlor. He and Shirley were ready to begin, and I made my last request as a single man: Can we wait until this inning is over? They did, we were wed and went out afterward to a local chain restaurant for a Reuben sandwich. Heaven forbid that we miss lunch!

In the meantime I had become more heavily involved with the Bob Hope Show at NBC, since bandleader and conductor Les Brown was not of the mind to attend all the necessary pre-production meetings. Les was an avid golfer and country club denizen who hated to spend time at a TV studio when he could be enjoying himself in other ways. The top brass at NBC determined that Hope's ratings were far better whenever he did a show on location, as opposed to one done locally at the NBC studios. They informed the producer of that fact, and advised him to plan out-of-town venues for the upcoming Hope specials. When Les heard that news, he told them he would only go if he could take his entire band of regulars with him. This didn't sit all that well with the producer due to the huge cost factor. Les then told NBC the best bet was to take me as conductor with about five key players and use local musicians to fill out the band. I was informed of this in 1973, and didn't think too much of the challenge since I'd done so many Hope shows and knew the protocol. So, we took off in a jet aircraft furnished by the F.A.A. from Los Angeles to Baltimore, where I conducted a live telethon hosted by Hope. I found a pretty decent bunch of players in Baltimore, and the show came off without a hitch.

From that point forward, this became more of a normal pattern than an exception. I ended up at army bases, as well as some of the more rewarding locales: Hawaii, Australia, Tahiti, London, Paris, Stockholm plus numerous locations throughout the United States. Hope loved playing military bases and we did them from coast to coast and all points in between. He had annual birthday celebrations that were two and three hour television extravaganzas, with famous stars to help celebrate his birthdays, starting with his 75th and continuing on yearly until his shows came to a close in 1993. Some shows were done from the Kennedy Center in Washington, D.C., with the President in attendance. I recall doing a three-hour show with Ronald Reagan in the balcony. Aside from the normal security checks, all the musicians including myself were patted down by the secret service for concealed weaponry, plus we were sniffed by explosive-detecting guard dogs as we entered the orchestra pit. They informed us that once we were seated, we could not leave until the president was safely out of the building at the conclusion of the performance.

"What if one of us has to use the bathroom?" I asked one of the agents.

"You go in your pants!" was the response.

At that time, Reagan was still in a state of paranoia from the attack by John Hinkley, so the security was beefed up to an almost laughable extent. Secret service people with their two-way talkback systems were in the pit along with the orchestra. As if the stress wasn't enough to have sixteen major acts to conduct in a three-hour show, airing **live** at the time, I had these secret service folks to contend with as well. However, we pulled it off without a hitch and went on to the next show. At the end of that episode, I returned to my room at the Watergate Hotel, called room service for a bottle of scotch and proceeded to relax myself into a sense of much-needed relief. Always being aware of the pitfalls of excessive drinking, I found that I could hold about three drinks of hard liquor with comfort. I don't go past that point for the sake of not wanting to lose control. The many years of family confrontations were always a specter in my subconscious.

When I initially began as a music arranger for the Bob Hope Specials, I would guess that Hope was in his early to mid sixties. He was still "Rapid Robert," flinging out his standard cadenced jokes faster than the audience could absorb them. He was an avid golfer, a constant world traveler and as always, envisioned himself as a ladies man, as he was in his 40s "Road to (?)" film series with Bing Crosby and Dorothy Lamour, and as a comic lover in "Paleface" with Jane Russell.

My start with the Hope organization began in 1970, and finished in 1993, when I had elected to leave the pressurized zone of Hollywood showbiz. By the time I had decided to take the pension and head back to the east coast, Hope was about eighty-eight years of age, and his shows trimmed to about two per year by NBC. His ratings had waned, and his senses were severely impaired. His eyesight was so bad that the cue cards had letters almost the size of those on a theatre marquee. His hearing was almost totally gone, and he was too vain to wear a hearing aid. On one special, toward the end of the show he thanked Bob Albertenelli for the music. This was after I'd been doing the show for seven years. I didn't recognize the name, so I never turned around to take my bow. Before the show aired, Hope was brought back in to the studio to re-record my name properly.

Bob's hearing loss led to uncomfortable problems for me. We would usually pre-record the music background tracks the day before, and when the show would actually be done in front of a live audience, we would play the tracks back to the stage at a reasonable level as an accompaniment, so that Bob could sing live to the pre-recorded background music. The normal playback level wasn't anywhere near loud enough for him to discern where the rhythm was, and he kept drifting a beat or two away. We'd have to stop and do it over repeatedly. In a case such as that, the track couldn't be played any louder because it would enter the live mike, which was picking up his vocal, causing audio overload, distortion and feedback.

That dilemma created a new facet for my job. I would have to station myself in front of the center camera, under the cue cards, and while kneeling down, hand signal Hope on each line. A downbeat meant, "start," a hand up, palm facing outward meant, "wait." I would do this with each song we videotaped probably for the last five years of the show. Occasionally Hope would still drift away and usually blame me for his miscue. Obviously, he was extremely frustrated, as was I. This is what's known in the industry as *The Eddie Fisher Syndrome*. When Fisher was at the height of his popularity in the '50s, he had a TV show sponsored by Coca-Cola. Eddie had, and probably still has, a huge problem with *meter* in music. He never could sense how many beats to hold any given note, or how many beats to wait before starting the next line of a song. During his shows that were performed on live TV, someone always had to be stationed under the camera cueing him on every line, when to begin a phrase and when to stop. I had the opportunity to act as an interim conductor for Fisher in 1971, so I know whence I speak.

I never developed a personal relationship with Bob. I don't know if anyone ever did. He was basically the same as almost every star in the biz; egocentric, self-serving and in his case, very tight with a buck. Many were the times I'd have to do battle over small items like a five-dollar cab fare. Once while doing a Hope show in New York, I had finished the recording session at midnight on New York's west side, near Times Square, and I had to deliver the master tapes to the video post-production studio at 43rd Street and First Avenue. It was a rainy night and, as luck would have it, I managed to hail an empty cab. Upon entering the studio, I handed the tapes to the on-duty audio engineer and entered the video room where Hope was sitting with associate producer Silvio Caranchini. I gave Silvio the cab receipt for $5.70, as it was his job to reimburse us for paid out expenses. Hope happened to glance over at it from the adjacent chair and muttered,

"What's that?"

"Alberti's cab fare," responded Sil.

"For Christ sake!" said Hope. "There's a cross-town bus on 42nd Street. What the Hell did you have to take a cab for?"

I almost laughed, thinking it was his sense of humor. However, I could tell by the expression on his face that he wasn't joking. It took about a month, but I finally got reimbursed. Hope insisted on personally screening and signing every check for petty cash.

Hope's tight-fisted fiscal exploits are legendary. One anecdote that has been around tells about one of his production meetings. He always had a staff of comedy writers on salary, which in his eyes gave him the right to call them at any hour of the day or night and have a meeting. This particular time, he'd called a meeting at his house in Toluca Lake, California at 9:00 AM Sunday. The six writers arrived to find Hope having a sumptuous breakfast at the big round-table where the meetings were usually held in his sunroom. He began listing his ideas and demands, never offering the bleary-eyed, half-awake writers so much as a cup of coffee. He went on eating and talking, until his houseman came in and told him he had a phone call. He arose from the table and went into his office to take the call. A few minutes later when he returned to the table, the plate was empty and his breakfast had disappeared. The writers had eaten it. Without batting an eye, he simply continued the meeting.

The positive aspect of my employment with this group was that I was in on every show from the first production meeting until the night the show aired. I came up with musical ideas, wrote medleys for Hope to sing with guest artists, arranged all the music, conducted shows and spent time laying in cue music in the post-production studios. This would amount to about six weeks for each show, and I would charge hourly union wages for every minute of my time. Since NBC made out the paychecks, it was a chance to make a nice piece of change, while having chunks added to my pension fund. When it all began, we were doing about six or seven shows a year. Toward the end, when it had dwindled to only one or two, the financial reward was not nearly enough to keep me interested. Additionally, the routines that Hope was willing to perform were all remakes of previous skits from shows in years past. He'd simply update names and places but the skits were stale. At that time he wasn't able to learn new routines. The audiences were of a different generation and his brand of humor was not being well received as it had been during World War II and the Korean conflict. The youth rebellion of the '70s placed Hope in a position of hawkishness during Vietnam, and this kept a segment of the audience from appreciating his attempts at humor. He had a fascination and adoration of politicians (usually right-wingers) and military top brass. His humor was largely politically skewed, and in times when polarization was pulling the factions apart, his audience dwindled. Toward the end of my reign with Hope, he'd be reading jokes off the cue cards, and would feign a laugh as a cue to the audience that the joke was over. At the same time, he'd often have a quizzical look, which led some of us to surmise that he didn't get the meaning of the joke either. It was rather sad and difficult to watch.

Some of the positives of my tenure as music director on the Hope show were the multitude of foreign and exotic lands I got to visit. Among them I can count Tahiti, Hawaii, Australia, London, Paris, Stockholm and Mexico as being memorable. Unfortunately, everything didn't always go as planned with our shows. The one from Stockholm was to be performed the same day that the Swedish Prime Minister, Olaf Palme was assassinated. The whole time Hope was doing one-liners to a somber audience, the King and Queen were in a theatre box, sobbing throughout the entire performance. The country was in mourning and Hope was trying to be humorous. Somehow, the old show-biz phrase, *"It went over like a lead balloon"* applied that day.

We did shows from every military base imaginable, both domestic and foreign. West Point, Annapolis, Pensacola and Colorado Springs were favorites of Hope since the attendees were all military trainees or military brass. He loved to stay at the Generals' Quarters on major military installations and be entertained and regaled by the officers in charge. Once we did a show on board the *USS Iwo Jima,* an aircraft carrier that was anchored in New York Harbor. In the initial preparations, it was suggested to Bob that they order sandbags to put around the base of the TV cameras, since it was more than likely a strong wind would arise during the taping. In his penny-wise, pound-foolish way he refused to pay for sandbags. As predicted, a strong breeze came along mid-day and a $40,000 TV camera ended up in the Hudson River.

Many of the same people were part of the Hope show throughout all the years it was on the air. Barney McNulty was the cue card person. He and his crew had every word scripted on three sets of cue cards, one set directly beside the center camera, one set to camera right and the other to camera left. The standing joke among us was that Barney slept under Hope's bed with a cue card that read, "Good morning, Dolores." For some reason, Hope relied totally on cue cards. As the years progressed, his eyesight became very poor and the lettering on the cards had to get progressively larger. The last couple of years of production, the letters looked like they'd fit on a theatre marquee.

Another crewmember was prop man Al Borden, who began with Hope during the radio days when Bob had a weekly show sponsored by Pepsodent toothpaste. He was there for the duration of the TV shows up until about 1990, when age and arthritis forced him to retire. Al was the "goat" for everything that went wrong with props used in the skits, and more often than not, they **did** go wrong. I recall a hillbilly skit we did with Hope and Glen Campbell, where at the end, a box was to open and a live chicken was to flutter out. Al Borden neglected to put air holes in the box, and consequently a dead chicken flopped out onto Hope's lap. Many a time we had to stop tape in order for Al to waddle across the stage and get heckled by Hope for something that didn't work right. Al Borden was the personification of *Murphy's Law*.

All things considered, I felt the end of Hope's career was close at hand, and the TV industry had completely eschewed the variety format. This meant that there was no place for me to go when his series was over. MTV had replaced the earlier variety show format with videos of current rock and rap stars. For those of us who had been a part of the network studio orchestra era, the party was over. It had been a glorious period in the golden age of television, and as I reflected upon it I felt extremely fortunate to have had contact with all the great people in the entertainment industry that my chosen profession brought about.

CHAPTER 16

WHERE TO GO FROM HERE?

It's hard to imagine the feeling when one's lifelong profession is no longer in demand. With the rapid change in public tastes and the advent of technology, no line of work is secure. The television music business proved to be no exception. Programs now used synthesizers or electronic sound effects rather than orchestral scores as themes, and the proponents of electronic wizardry were rapidly replacing the music masters in the studios.

I admit to feeling that the world was passing me by, and with Los Angeles being the trendiest area in the nation, even my talents as a pianist were not especially welcomed by the listening public. In order to be accepted in L.A., a pianist had to be at the vanguard of jazz, such as Herbie Hancock or Chick Corea, and since I was from the earlier swing/jazz school with my early influences being Teddy Wilson, Oscar Peterson, et al, I wasn't much in demand. I saw little if any future remaining for my career in the southern California area.

To make my state of mind even gloomier, I felt as if Los Angeles had evolved into a third-world city, with gang members numbering well into the thousands, as one ethnic or racial group banded together to thwart the power of another. Graffiti was scrawled over most of the city, including the nicer bedroom communities within the sprawling complex of L.A. The once quiet nights were now constantly being pierced by the sounds of police helicopters hovering overhead with high-powered searchlights scanning the ground for escaping felons. Sirens from police vehicles and ambulances broke the normal ambience throughout daylight and nighttime hours. The freeways were filled to the point of gridlock with so-called rush hour now encompassing most daylight hours. This was adding to the ever-present brownish-gray sky color, which brought to mind scenes from the film "Soylent Green," a depressing view of a major city in the next century.

I was sleeping more and enjoying life less. Thoughts of how to escape the area and become productive once again were constantly trickling through my consciousness, although most seemed impractical and quite elusive. At one point I considered Australia since I knew of a thriving orchestral industry in Sydney, but the circumstances were not right for a move of that magnitude. I had to come up with a *plan B* in order to protect my sanity. I knew the days of big pop orchestras were numbered, so I felt my best route was to find someplace where I could ply my first love, piano-playing.

Meanwhile, my mother was still unhappily married to Joe von Rottkay and living in a condominium in Boca Raton, Florida. Periodically, she'd announce that she was coming out to California for a visit, and whether or not it was at an opportune time for Shirley and me, when she made up her mind to do something it was a done deal. Most of her time was spent sitting in a chair in our living room, sipping vodka on the rocks, smoking long, dark-brown cigarettes and coughing. Her need to be an authoritarian figure made her assume a rather regal air, which was, I felt, a hollow attempt to overcome the feelings of inadequacy she'd held throughout her life.

Once, while our weekly housekeeper was busily dusting the living room, my mother snapped her fingers at the young girl, and said,

"Draw me a bath."

No please, no thank you, no niceness. I bristled!

Immediately I arose, grabbed a pencil and pad and proceeded to hastily scribble a likeness of a bathtub, with two faucets marked "hot" and "cold."

"Here!" I shouted. "This is a bath! You just turn the hot and the cold on, then get in and wash yourself! Or would you rather have one of the servants do that for you as well?"

This led to another blow-up between us, which was nothing new. It had been happening since my earliest recollection of childhood. Ultimately, she cut her visit short and returned to Boca Raton, probably with tales of what a bastard her son was.

Once in about 1985, Shirley and I were watching a women's tennis tournament on television. The site of the match was Hilton Head Island, South Carolina, and there was a hovering blimp with a TV camera attached that was showing beauty shots of the area. It looked so inviting; I suggested to Shirley that we look into a vacation there the following year, one to coincide with the tournament. We called the Hilton Head Chamber of Commerce, and they were quick to send a pictorial book with all the local businesses and hotels listed. Since Shirley had never traveled to that part of the country I suggested that we make Hilton Head the first stop, then travel by car to Myrtle Beach, Williamsburg, and on up to New York. We set our itinerary accordingly.

In 1986, as our vacation time rolled around we flew to Savannah, Georgia where we rented a car to drive to Hilton Head. It's about a 45-minute drive if you know the way, or about an hour-and-a-half for those of us who weren't used to the unlit lowcountry roads. We proceeded to check into a newly opened spectacular beachside hotel, The Intercontinental. The smell of the air, the ocean breeze and the general ambience of the island overwhelmed my senses. I fell in love with the area immediately.

Unfortunately, we only had three days before we were due to move on up the coast to Myrtle Beach, and I regretted the fact that we'd diversified our two weeks as much as we had. Since I'd not seen the other spots, I was expecting equally positive vibes. That soon came to a screeching halt as we checked in to a beachfront hotel in Myrtle Beach. The town was the antithesis of Hilton Head, and the streets were lined with amusement parks, T-shirt shops, tattoo parlors and topless bars. Finding a decent restaurant was nearly impossible, and we both agreed after one night to cancel the remaining days there and move on. The beauty of Hilton Head was still in our blood

Williamsburg, Virginia was picturesque and quaint, and we explored the area as best we could, despite the fact that it rained the whole time we were there. Scenically it was lovely, but I could see myself becoming reclusive from boredom if we moved there. We spent a couple of days in Williamsburg and then moved on northward for the remainder of the vacation.

We returned to Los Angeles which by then looked worse than ever to me, smelled raunchier and seemed more crowded than when we left. The terminal at LAX International Airport reminded me of the canteen scene in "Star Wars." Strange creatures with green and orange spiked hair, tattooed bodies and pierced body parts seemed to abound. A multitude of cultures could be seen, but I didn't seem to fit into any of them. My heart was still in Hilton Head.

That fall, we made plans to return for another vacation, only this time spending an entire week on Hilton Head. Upon settling in on our vacation, an event occurred that would forever change our lives. We'd been walking the beach, wandering past the marinas and taking in the friendly feelings that accompanied the expansive green forests. We stopped somewhere for dinner, and then returned to the Intercontinental. I noticed a sign in the lobby that advertised a jazz trio in the Gazebo Lounge, a beautifully appointed circular room with walls of glass overlooking the pool and beach. We went in, were seated, ordered a couple of rounds, and were relaxing when the waitress informed us that there would be a delay in the music. Apparently the regular pianist took a night off and the substitute pianist had not shown up. Although I was wearing a touristy sweatshirt with *Hilton Head* emblazoned across the front, I asked her to tell the existing musicians that there was a "half-baked piano player" in the audience who would be willing to help fill in until the sub arrived.

After a brief conversation with the bassist, who was in a tuxedo and the female vocalist who was beautifully gowned, they agreed to let me play a tune. Not a set, but a tune, which is par for the course. As far as they were concerned I could have been a total dud, and after one song, they could have said thanks and kissed me off. However, they soon realized that I was a pro. I continued to play....and play...and play. The sub never showed up so I did the entire evening. I can't tell you how much I enjoyed that night, reveling in the fact that the audience was most appreciative of my type of music.

The following day I had a phone call from the regular pianist who thanked me for saving the evening and insisted on paying me, since I was the actual sub. He also asked if I'd be willing to play that Friday since he had another job and needed someone to cover the Gazebo job. I happily agreed and said I'd be sure to wear something more apropos than a sweatshirt.

Friday evening I joined the others in the Gazebo, and was surprised to find a large number of local folk sitting around the music area. As it turned out, they were from a recently formed jazz society on Hilton Head and came in to hear the new piano player on the island. Word travels rapidly in Hilton Head, and it seemed that everyone who had an interest in the local music scene was on hand. After the first set, they introduced themselves in a most gracious manner, welcoming Shirley and me to the island, and to their homes as well. The beginning of a new social set had taken root. I was glad to know there was an interest in music, (especially jazz) and also tennis, which was one of Shirley's main avocations. As far as I was concerned, I could pack in Los Angeles the following week and move to Hilton Head.

Selling Shirley on this idea was another story. After all, she had a good paying position at Paramount Studios in Hollywood as Script Supervisor on "Entertainment Tonight," and along with it an excellent health plan that covered the both of us. Her identity was totally wrapped up in the show and the importance that accompanied her position, a situation to which I could relate and understand. Actually the pressure of the job was taking a toll both physically and mentally on her, but she was too involved to see that. Standing on the outside, I could see the migraine headaches becoming more frequent, the body aches and pains showing up more often, and the stress level gaining as the years went by. As for any good, competent and conscientious person, her job took on an importance beyond reality. Having to wake up at 4:30 AM in order to be on the job at 6:15 five days a week meant napping at 5 in the afternoon, and hitting the hay for real at about 8 o'clock in the evening after unwinding at dinner. Our social life was restricted to only dining out on Sunday nights usually with another couple, Bob & Shelley Mills. Bob was one of Hope's gag writers and Shelley was Shirley's tennis partner every Saturday morning.

Shirley was very aware of my growing unrest and discontent with the path of the music industry, and I know she felt empathetic toward my feelings. As I was faced with more time off due to the decreasing number of television shows that had live music, I began to retreat more often to Hilton Head, to get away from an environment in which I felt more detached every day. One problem was the cost of hotel rooms. Since the island was a resort the escalating hotel rates were prohibitive, so we felt some sort of adjustment had to be made.

In 1987, we once again embarked on a vacation to Hilton Head. It was September, and after a week on the island, we planned on heading to Boca Raton to visit my mother and stepfather. I'd noticed in a real estate booklet on Hilton Head that there were a great number of condos and villas for sale. The idea occurred to me that we could purchase a condo, rent it out in high season and still use it for our vacations during the slack times. This would nullify much of the cost of hotels, and it would give me a sense of having at least one foot in the direction that I wanted to go. We chose a friendly realtor who showed us a number of places, and one in particular we liked because of its beachfront location. After mulling it over with Shirley, we thought we'd make a low-ball offer to the owner, a doctor in Dallas, Texas. We wrote up the offer on a Sunday and decided to have it submitted the following day. Shirley and I departed the island on Monday bound for Boca Raton with an intermediate stopover in Daytona Beach. As we checked in at our Daytona hotel, a message was waiting from our realtor. It said, in essence, "He took the offer. The condo is yours."

We immediately ran for the cocktail lounge, ordered a stiff one, and wondered what we had done! We owned a villa in Hilton Head, and we didn't even remember what it looked like! Nonetheless, this was one of the best deals we'd ever made. That Monday turned out to be the infamous "Black Monday" in 1987 when the stock market crashed. The owner had been heavily invested on margin, and needed the cash from the sale of the villa, which apparently was why our bid was accepted so rapidly without even a counter offer.

Having a piece of property on Hilton Head, we kept finding more and more reasons to fly cross-country for renovations, redecoration or just for fun. I found myself spending a lot more time there, if for no other reason, just to familiarize myself with the area, the people and the lifestyle, which was quite different from Los Angeles. Each time I had to pack up and return to L.A., I became more anxious to make the island my full-time permanent home.

The years went on, the work in Los Angeles kept decreasing, and the societal unrest between ethnic and racial groups seem to be compounding in southern California. It was ultimately the horrific beating of motorist Rodney King by the Los Angeles police sparking riots that spilled over into our neighborhood that scared the daylights out of us. Shirley was told to leave work at Paramount, and that the studio would completely close down until further notice. That was the first time since its inception it had ever closed, even through World War II. In driving home to our condo in the San Fernando Valley, Shirley had to drive over the sidewalk near Sunset Boulevard in order to avoid street rioters. Buildings were burning, store windows were being smashed, and drivers were being pulled from stopped cars and trucks, only to be beaten by rioting mobs. A curfew was put on all vehicles as of five o'clock in the afternoon.

We had endured the Watts riots in the mid-sixties, the gruesome Manson multiple murders, the Patty Hearst debacle with the S.L.A. in the mid-seventies, and now this. The others were miles away but this one ended up affecting our neighborhood, as well as our feeling of safety and security. We had planned on having a pizza that evening at a restaurant about a mile away, but with the curfew on autos our only alternative was to walk. As we slowly strode down Ventura Boulevard, the smell of lingering smoke from burning buildings hung heavily in the air. There were shards of broken glass along the sidewalks and the victimized storefronts were boarded up. I was once again reminded of scenes in the movie, "On The Beach," seeing a normally thriving metropolitan thoroughfare devoid of moving vehicles, and virtually no pedestrians other than us. As we approached the restaurant, for the first time, Shirley said, "Maybe it's time to pack it in and get out of here." I couldn't have agreed more. I also had a premonition about a very large earthquake that added to my desire to leave. Ten months after moving away from Los Angeles one actually occurred, rendering our condo uninhabitable.

After having our pizza, still feeling shaken by the day's events, I somehow felt a sense of calm as I realized that we were in accord about leaving a city that had outlived its usefulness in our lives, and we now could plan to put *plan B* into action.

CHAPTER 17

CALIFORNIA, THERE WE GO

Moving is never easy, and relocating coast-to-coast is even more arduous. The logistics were overwhelming to say the least, and we had been planning months in advance. I'd rented a storage locker in Van Nuys, California, where I brought cartons of items such as L.P. records, books, score pads, and things that I could do without for the time period. We were trying to ease our burden when the actual moving day arrived.

To exacerbate matters, the expected phone call came late one night while I was asleep. My mother had died earlier that evening of a combination of ailments. Lung cancer, emphysema and cirrhosis of the liver were the primary causes. Diabetes and alcoholism were major factors although they were not listed on the official death certificate. I flew to Boca Raton to calm down Joe von Rottkay who by now was in early stages of dementia. Upon arriving, he confronted me with accusations that I'd stripped his bank account, and that he was broke. The reality was I didn't even know where his bank account was. This was definitely an early sign of his weakened state, being eighty-four at the time, ten years older than my mother. Joe died about eight months afterward, with his dementia in full swing. I then had to spend about a month clearing up the estate in Florida. I sold the condo, gave away most of their belongings to charities and with a certain sense of closure and relief, returned to California.

A few people came to look at our condominium in Studio

City after we had listed it for sale. The realtors showed up by the dozens at open-house day, knowing that there was going to be a free catered lunch. The real estate market was a bit slack in the early '90s, and things weren't moving that well. One potential condo seeker was a Hollywood actress, who arrived accompanied by her psychic guru. To some, this might seem a bit off-the-wall, but if you lived in and around *la-la-land* long enough, it wouldn't come as a surprise. The psychic lady walked from room to room, exclaiming,

"I feel love in this place."

We echoed her remarks, assuring her that there certainly was more than enough love within those walls. We omitted the part about the crotchety neighbors directly below us, and the fact that the folks overhead had installed a marble floor that magnified each and every footstep.

About a week later, the realtor came by and told us this actress wanted the place. We had asked what we considered to be fair market value, but knowing the softness of the market we gladly accepted about eight percent below our asking price. The catch was she wanted occupancy in thirty days. We wanted sixty, but the deal hinged upon her ability to gain almost immediate occupancy. Our answer was a definite "yes."

The following morning, I grabbed a flight to Hilton Head with one thing in mind: find a house to rent. The first one the rental agent showed me was quite pleasant but the master bedroom had what appeared to be some hand painted green ooze at the ceiling line. It was reminiscent of a campy sci-fi flick, where an alien entered through the cracks. I was told that I wasn't allowed to repaint, so I eliminated that one from the realm of possibilities. Nightmares would have abounded!

The next one was a lovely place on Oyster Reef Drive, and I agreed to take it. The owners were in New Jersey and the current tenant was in the last month of his lease. It would be a tight turnaround, but I figured we could make it happen. I called Shirley and gave her the good news, then grabbed a flight back to Los Angeles. Although we already owned a condo on Hilton Head, it was fully furnished and was rented well in advance, so it was not someplace we could count on staying. We didn't want to buy in a panic, so a rental house for one year seemed like the most logical step.

Now the crunch really hit. We had to get estimates from movers, as well as auto transport companies. It's amazing how much clutter we accumulated. The next month was solidly consumed with packing and planning. Transferring funds to a bank in South Carolina, moving the brokerage accounts, undoing the utilities in Los Angeles and establishing accounts with those in South Carolina were only a few of the chores we faced.

Moving day arrived in what seemed like an hour, although in reality it was four weeks later. The realtor gave us the cashier's check; the moving van arrived, as did the transport vehicle that moved our cars across country. The vehicles were loaded on the top of the multi car carrier, and they were now in the trust of the driver, whom we would eventually meet up with in our new home. The big hitch was that on the day we were to fly to Hilton Head, there were no airplane reservations to be had. It was tourist season, and the Family Circle tennis tournament was in full swing. We had to wait three extra days before we could embark on our flight to Hilton Head, which meant we had to book a hotel room at the Sportsmen's Lodge in Studio City and rent a car to boot. During those final three days in Los Angeles, many of our friends bought us farewell dinners and regaled us, all the while wondering what on earth we were going to do on some island in the Atlantic after half a lifetime in *Glitzville*. I often wondered as well, but I had a good hunch about the life move, so I didn't panic. Things would work out; I was sure of that.

When the day came to leave for Los Angeles International Airport, I hired a chauffeured limo to take us there in style. I also bought two first-class one-way tickets. It would have been a great deal less costly if I'd bought round trip tickets and used only the first part, but the symbolism was extremely important to me. I'd wanted to leave the West Coast for a number of years, and this meant that I was finally getting my wish.

As we checked in to U. S. Airways, I was gleefully shouting,

"I'm out'a here! One way! I'm gone!"

I'm sure nobody even offered a second glance at my victory dance since this airport was full of loonies. The airport was filled with tattooed people sporting pierced body parts and all sorts of other strange forms of humanity. This was a large part of the strong desire I had to leave the southern California vicinity. As a traditional dresser and a man of fundamental values, I felt like an alien in a foreign land. The trendiness of the entertainment industry was something I always despised, and as time went on I had a very difficult time buying basic clothing. The largest pants waist size in any department store was a thirty-four, and that was considered obese. If you weren't anorexic or built like a surfer you'd have a very difficult time buying clothes. One young salesman in a department store once told me, as I asked about a pair of trousers in my size,

"Yeah, we had one size thirty-six, but that old guy over there (pointing to a senior salesclerk) took 'em"

I wasn't about to personally embark on a new fashion path of wearing T-shirts with obscenities on them and tie-dyed tattered jeans. One thing that struck me as a plus for the Hilton Head area: I could buy clothes that fit me! I was also among people who looked pretty much the same as me, which made it a lot more comfortable, and gave me a sense of belonging.

The flight took off on time, and even though it was eleven o'clock in the morning, a Bloody Mary was quickly in hand to toast the end of an era. I've always believed that it's important to make some changes in lifestyle periodically. I was a New Yorker for the first twenty-five years of my life, a Californian for the next thirty-four and here we were, off to South Carolina, a southern state that definitely was not considered the *Deep South*. It was a relatively poor state, with the exception of a couple of coastal areas, namely Charleston and Hilton Head. Once a person crossed the bridge to Hilton Head they had the sense of leaving the south and entering a land populated primarily by northerners and upper midwestern folk. Those changes always sparked a new sense of feeling alive, shedding the ennui that had settled in over the past couple of decades in Los Angeles.

Our first stop after renting a car was our condo at the Island Club, which luckily was vacant for three days until the next renter was due to check in. We dined out that evening, toasting our new move and proceeded to await the arrival of the moving van and our cars from California. They all got there, with the cars arriving first. The driver needed a cashier's check in order to unload them from his transport vehicle. Since it was six-thirty in the morning, we knew the local bank wouldn't be open until nine, so we had to wait that one out. The transaction went smoothly, and the cars were undamaged, albeit caked with sand and mud from the cross-country trip.

Shortly thereafter, the moving van arrived. The driver had picked up some local helpers in Savannah, and once we gave him the green light they began to unload the cartons. We had carefully marked each carton with the room to which it belonged, but that didn't seem to matter as the ones marked "Kitchen" were ending up in the bedroom, the den, and all over. As we found out, the helpers were illiterate, and couldn't read the large room markings, so our job was to catch them as they entered the house and verbally instruct them as to the destination of each box.

I mentioned things would be tight, and they were. The tenants who had occupied the house had hoped to be out a week earlier and into the new home they had built. There were construction delays and, as a result they were moving their belongings out just as our van drove up. Needless to say there was no time for a cleaning crew to come in and give the rental house a thorough once-over before we unloaded our belongings. Fortunately for us, the previous tenants were immaculately clean, leaving very little for us to deal with that day.

Settling in to a new environment takes a while, and this move was no exception. We knew that the rental was to be a temporary dwelling until such time when we would find the home we'd choose to purchase, or build, as the case may be.

Most of the items that were not necessities such as books, record albums and extra culinary utensils stayed packed in cartons, and were stored in an air-conditioned facility. Now that we had our own bed once again, my thoughts began to turn to the world of music, and Shirley's to hooking up with some tennis partners.

A musician friend once told me that everything I touch seems to turn to gold and that I seemed to attract good fortune. That prophecy seemed to continue (to this point,) as far as my entry into the music world on Hilton Head was concerned. Unfortunately, within six months prior to my arriving the two best jazz pianists in the area passed away. Joe Jones, a wonderful jazz artist and Kenny Palmer, a Savannah fixture who was a close associate of Johnny Mercer, both developed cancer and died away within one year. This left a huge hole in the local music community, which unknowingly, I was destined to fill. I couldn't play hard-driving jazz and funk as Joe Jones could, nor could I drink as much as either Joe or Kenny. My expectations were that I might sub or fill in for someone a couple of times a month. Instead, I ended up filling a big portion of the slots left vacant by the untimely deaths of those two fine musicians. Truly a sad circumstance.

Although the life of a studio musician in Los Angeles has many disadvantages, one nice part of it is anonymity. Other than one's peers, nobody on the outside knows what you do for a living. I could go almost anywhere and not be recognized, which to my somewhat withdrawn privacy-seeking psyche was great. I hadn't anticipated a 180-degree turnaround when I made the move to Hilton Head. The musicians union in Hollywood had in excess of 13,000 members, and we were simply a part of the working community, not celebrities.

I hadn't been here a month before a Savannah television station called and asked if they could send a camera crew over to do an interview. The local newspaper, *The Island Packet* followed suit with a spread proclaiming, "Nationally famous pianist makes island his home." The idea of having a relaxed period of my life in voluntary semi-retirement had taken a different path than I had anticipated. The status of *celebrity* had unwittingly been bestowed upon me, mostly due to my long association with Bob Hope. The *"big fish in a small pond"* syndrome had sunk in, putting me in a position that I had never before experienced. Normally quiet shopping at a supermarket now became a conversation pit. I'd had my picture and name splattered over so many pages of the local press that the island residents felt they all knew me. They had one name to learn, I had thousands. Not possessing the greatest memory for names, it took me a long time to absorb the names of the multitude of new friends and a few fans, many of who were aficionados of good music and/or Bob Hope.

One organization that has a chapter on Hilton Head is U.N.I.C.O., an Italian-American group dedicated to raising funds for scholarships and keeping the image of Italians in a positive light. They're mostly businessmen and restaurateurs, and the nice part of belonging was a weekly luncheon held at an excellent down-home Sicilian-style bistro, *Fratello's*. The first year of our arrival on Hilton Head they decided to do a fundraiser in the form of a jazz concert and had approached me about participating. My first thought was clarinetist Buddy De Franco, a gem of a man and brilliant musician who lived in Florida. He would reflect positively on the image that U.N.I.C.O. wished to project, and after a call to him, he responded that he'd be happy to perform. I remembered having played with him in past years, and that brought to mind drummer Frank De Vito, an old buddy from L.A. and a former De Franco sideman. I called Frank, and he gladly accepted the offer to come out and play the concert, while staying with Shirley and me for a week at our home. Bassist Frank Duvall rounded out the quartet, which turned out to truly be a crowd-pleaser. The concert was a great success.

Having joined U.N.I.C.O., I met some business people from all walks of industry. At a dinner one evening, I mentioned that I was planning to record another CD, and that I was looking toward Atlanta as a possible area to do the project. One of the members suggested that I hold off for a little while, as he and another U.N.I.C.O. member had plans to build a studio on Hilton Head, and start a record company as well. This sounded like something I could wait for since recording locally would probably be less costly and generally more convenient.

About eight months later, Dolphin Studios was completed, having been designed by former Nashville studio owner Norbert Putnam. Norbert was willing to hang out for a bit and train the up-and-coming engineers with the technical operation. One day he asked if I could get a bassist and a drummer together to record, mainly to test the isolation booths for any sound leakage. I called Delbert Felix, one of the best local bassists around, who agreed to come by. One of our engineers was Mark Husbands, a full-time working drummer, and he was glad to supply his drum set and his talent to the testing project. A Yamaha C-7 conservatory grand piano had been handpicked from the concert pool and was ready for the first recording at Dolphin.

After listening to the first couple of jazz tunes we recorded, it dawned on me that we had the makings of the album I had hoped to do in Atlanta. I paid the two musicians and set up subsequent recording sessions, which eventually became "Nice 'n' Easy" with the Bob Alberti trio. It was released on the Dolphin label in 1995, and generated a good number of sales. Airplay helped the number of CDs sold, and the fact that some of the cuts were on the play list of *Music Choice,* a satellite and cable music network didn't hurt either. Every time one of the cuts aired, the title of the album and artist would pop up on the TV screen, and continued for about three years with their jazz channel.

Other artists began recording projects at Dolphin Studios, and being that I had more professional experience in the recording field than anyone in the area, I was constantly being tapped to provide back-up groups of musicians as well as arrangements. In fact, I was busier recording here than I was in Los Angeles, the recording capital of the country. So much for my retirement!

There was definitely a lack of professional musicians residing in the area. Supply and demand was in my favor as I was getting called for most jobs in Hilton Head and the Savannah area. Having had experience with the society bands in New York made my presence a bonus for the dances and parties that were hosted by people from my era. Having learned about two thousand show tunes and standards in order to work for the likes of Lester Lanin, Meyer Davis et al, I could fulfill just about any request. The local players were of varied levels of talent, but the one common thread was that very few of them had a repertoire that went past about thirty songs. The club date business was there for the taking, and I put in a great many evenings plying a trade I'd engaged in forty years earlier.

My ability to read music was another plus. Although I was never a classical player, I could handle shows, recording sessions and most types of reading tasks that were placed before me. Arranging also came into play; I was probably the only person in the area who had the experience of thirty-plus years in Hollywood, scoring TV shows and films, so at the times when those chores were needed, I was usually called. Artists who wanted to do CDs would contact me to put together the arrangements and hire the musicians. A good number of albums sprung forth from this little corner of the world.

In 1997, Bob Rada, the principal trombonist with the Hilton Head Orchestra contacted me. He came up with an idea to do pops concerts with various artists. These performances would act as fundraisers for the orchestra and bring another dimension to the local music scene. I agreed to be a participant, and the first concert we did was a tribute to Henry Mancini. I procured the Mancini library from a close friend in Hollywood, and a new annual event was born. I was then appointed Special Pops Conductor of the Orchestra, an honor I cherish to this day.

Needless to say, all these developments were much more than I had anticipated when we made our move to Hilton Head Island. I started to feel a sense of burnout, and that is a strange sensation for a musician. From our earliest days, musicians learn to say yes to every job offer, being that we never know when the next one will surface. Despite our sense of security as we mature this habit never seems to leave. I'm as guilty as anyone of being caught in that syndrome. In fact, I requested in my will that after I leave the bonds of earth, my remains be cremated and put in an hourglass, ostensibly so I can keep working. ("Turn Bob over; the eggs are done!")

Bob with legendary jazz guitarist, Barney Kessel
1992

Sharing a swingin' moment with renown saxophonist, Scott
Hamilton, 2000

The UNICO Jazz Festival got things jumpin' at the Crown Plaza resort for two nights straight. Jammin' at Monday evening's performance were (left to right) Bruce Spradley, Frank Duvall, Dick Goodwin, Carl Fontana, Peter Appleyard, Harry Allen and Bob Alberti on the piano.

CHAPTER 18

ONE MORE FOR THE ROAD

R inging telephones have always been an annoyance to me, and to this day, every time I'm forced to get out of a comfortable chair and pick up a phone call, I tend to spew out obscenities in a low grumbling voice as I prepare to say "Hello" in a reasonably pleasant tone.

It was sometime in 1997 that this muttering of obscenities was especially virulent. I was sitting in an easy chair on our screen porch with an iced tea, listening to the cable jazz channel. The shrill chirping of the phone disrupted my temporary nirvana. After a batch of expletives, I answered the phone sounding like a normal, happy individual. The caller was an old acquaintance, Steve Lawrence, half of the "Steve & Eydie" team with spouse Eydie Gorme. After we exchanged pleasantries, I waited to see what prompted him to call. As the conversation progressed, he said that he'd been in a restaurant in Las Vegas and heard a trio playing on the sound system. He asked the owner whose CD it was, and the answer was the Bob Alberti trio. This must have rung a bell with him, since I'd known them from various television shows throughout the years in Los Angeles. Then the real crux of the matter surfaced. Their pianist of over twenty years had left to work with singer Natalie Cole, and they were trying to find a replacement. Steve wanted to know if I'd be interested in joining them.

I hesitated to fully commit, but I said that depending on the frequency of their time on the road and the financial consideration I'd think about it. As it turned out, the reason their pianist jumped ship was because Steve & Eydie weren't working enough to support him, his lifestyle and his alimony payments. For me, the less time away from home, the better. Steve said they didn't do more than about 40 to 50 days a year of performing, which sounded reasonable. He said he'd have their manager, Judy Tannen call me and discuss the terms.

The sound of that name brought chills to my entire being. I'd mentioned two female managers with whom I'd dealt, (Helen Noga with Johnny Mathis and Barbara Belle with Keely Smith) and this woman was cut from the same cloth. Her basic disposition was usually negatively confrontational and her vocabulary was straight from the gutter. The thought of dealing with her was a definite minus in the entire equation. Nonetheless, the music that Steve & Eydie performed was wonderful to the ear and enjoyable to play. Musical giants such as Don Costa, Nelson Riddle, Marion Evans, Nick Perito among others had arranged most of their music library.

The first engagement I played with Steve and Eydie in 1997 was in Atlantic City. I had not been there in many years, and I remembered it from the 1950's when it was primarily a convention town. I used to play automobile shows at the beginning of the model year. Car companies would invite all their respective dealers to a display of the newest versions of their cars, and put on a gala show during the course of the convention. It was in Atlantic City prior to her marriage to Steve that I first played for Eydie when she appeared on one of the shows as a relatively new and obscure singer.

Subsequent engagements included Caesars Palace in Las Vegas, The Nugget in Reno and a number of concert venues in various major markets throughout the country. Florida was always a destination in February, as we would cover cities on both the east and west coasts of that state.

I had not been apprised of how the stage would be set up for their performance and was surprised to see that the concert grand piano was placed in front of the orchestra, adjacent to the conductor's podium. This put me in a direct line with the follow-spotlights, and those looked like a Boeing 747 coming in for a landing. Each one was the equivalent of 32,000 watts of illumination, and there were three of those hitting the stage at once. I found myself in the spotlight more than I cared to be, and I always had to look interested and amused. That wasn't always easy, especially as time marched on and I heard the same material over and over again.

The part of the act that kept me in a state of hyper-alertness was the last half hour of their act, where everything would be ad-lib. Steve and Eydie would perch themselves on barstools at the piano, banter back and forth and break into various songs without necessarily telling me what they were about to sing. One or the other would simply start singing something and I'd have to instantaneously assess the key (thank heaven for perfect pitch!) and accompany them on the piano, wherever the song happened to go. Luckily I have an extended memory bank of pop and show tunes, probably in excess of 2,000 melodies. I can't recall them ever starting a tune that I didn't know. Occasionally, Steve would make up a song, creating his own melody and lyrics as part of a humorous bit. I'd have to play it as if I actually knew it. I suppose this is where my value to the dynamic duo came into play.

The travel aspects were not quite as I had remembered from "the old days" of touring. The planes were bigger, but the seats were smaller. Airports had grown to humongous proportions, and the greatest dread was changing concourses in either Atlanta or Dallas-Ft. Worth. Since the musicians who were in the employ of Steve and Eydie came from all areas of the country, I was always on my own while I tried to make connecting flights with minimal time allocated to do so.

The time I spent working with the duo ran for about four years, until another phone call from Steve told me that they were canceling all further engagements because of Eydie's health problems. Eydie was a bit older than Steve, and having been a life-long cigarette smoker, her breath control could not be maintained to any reasonable level at this point in time. They had been doing less work with each successive year and by

2001, there had been only twenty performances for the entire year. I regretted the passing of an era; they were the last of the black-tie-and-gown acts still on the scene. However, the bright spot was that I'd probably never have to cross paths again with Judy Tannen. By this time, we coexisted by not speaking to one another.

Unfortunately, their purported "retirement" turned out to be other than the way it was presented to me. I believe the real kiss of death was my request for a salary increase. Since money has been and probably always will be God to Steve & Eydie, the request was looked upon as blasphemy of the first order. While they enjoyed multi-million dollar homes in Las Vegas and in Malibu, California, as well as a collection of priceless art and rare vintage wine, their long-term musicians had not gotten a raise in over ten years. The traveling accompanists knew that to ask for such an increase would result in being let go and had learned long ago to settle for the status quo. Steve & Eydie's company had always refused to pay into the musicians' pension plan, and also did not pay for travel days or any per diem for meals. With the engagements getting shortened down to two-day weekends, the resulting net salary became increasingly thin. Since I was in a fairly secure position and didn't especially care whether I worked with them or not, I risked my position by asking for a small increase. That apparently set the wheels in motion for them to groom a replacement pianist, one who was also willing to act as pianist/conductor. That way, they could also eliminate Jack Feierman, their conductor of twenty-seven years and save an extra salary. They followed the characteristics of most performers who I had encountered in my travels. You're their "great Buddy-Buddy" as long as they need you and can get you for a bargain, but as soon as that scenario is over, it's "Adios, Amigo." As a parting shot, they made sure that Jack Feierman and I were notified of our no longer being a part of the team just in time to negate our Christmas bonuses. Those funds could safely stay in the Lawrence's bank account gathering interest.

Performing with Steve & Eydie had some enjoyable side benefits since I was part of a group of musicians for whom I had great respect and an enjoyable social camaraderie. Among them were guitarist Al Caiola, one of the finest former studio musicians from New York, drummer Chuck Christiansen from Chicago, who was the glue that held the rhythm section together, trumpeter Bobby Hamilton from Las Vegas, and a dear old friend of mine with whom I'd played in my days at NBC in Burbank, conductor Jack Feierman. The friendships and enjoyable off-moments were the main counterbalance to my traveling trepidations as flying had become a nightmare.

The airlines had progressively cut amenities to the passengers and kept downsizing the seats. To get a thirty-six inch waist into a sixteen-inch seat was not exactly a joy, nor was the diet of soda and pretzels on a two-hour flight. In order to save money, Judy Tannen would book the musicians on the worst possible economy flights while she, Steve and Eydie flew by private luxury jet. This was all in the name of saving money for the company. I recall one engagement in Phoenix where I was routed from Savannah to Ft. Lauderdale to Houston to Phoenix, a trip that encompassed two different air carriers and three baggage changes. This trip could have been routed with one plane change, but they chose to use frequent flier miles in my name, which they pirated from all the trips I'd taken for them. My luggage was lost both going and coming. The return trip saw the suitcase arriving three days after I got home. This was typical of the business mindset of the organization. I was relieved to know that I wouldn't have to put up with that type of cattle-boat transportation any more.

In the two last engagements I had with Steve and Eydie, I realized what a compound hassle air travel had become. I reveled in the knowledge that after those two trips, I'd be able to avoid any mandatory travel, and could choose when and where I wanted to go, and how I selected to get there. The days of "Red-Carpet" service had long past, along with decent airline food. (An oxymoron, to say the least.) Gone were the days of cute, perky stewardesses. We now had wide-bodied aircraft and wide-bodied flight attendants. On one occasion, while in an aisle seat, I got thwacked every time one overly zaftig attendant strode up or down the aisle. At the same time, I had a morbidly obese gentleman in the center seat, and his excess was invading my seating space. My only defense was to lean toward the aisle, and in doing so, my shoulder was a prime target for the flight attendant's ample girth.

Although musicians were the Lawrences' life-blood, Judy Tannen made us out to be pariahs. I don't know what she had against musicians, but there was never any form of respect or friendliness shown, at least during my tenure. To add a little extra poison to the mix, their booking agent's ex-wife had run off with a saxophonist, so between the agent and the manager, you *know* that no special affection was shown to anyone holding a musician's union card. Judy would pass by in a hotel corridor or backstage, never acknowledging me or saying "hello." She would enter the stage area usually during the initial band rehearsal and proceed to scream unmercifully at stagehands, set decorators, coffee-servers and anyone within her sightline for the most minor infractions. The "F—word" was liberally used as a verb, adjective, adverb and pronoun to just about anyone with whom she came in contact. At one venue, the local stage manager would purposely take his vacation, making sure it coincided with the time that Steve and Eydie would be appearing. Tannen's power was far greater than it should have been, and she had worked her way up to being their manager, road representative, travel coordinator and personal secretary. Her tenure had been forty years at the time, and she had come from being a receptionist with one of their previous agents to full-time participant in every aspect of their lives. She nearly had live-in status in the Lawrence's former Beverly Hills estate, running the office from their home. Steve admittedly chose not to deal with personal conflicts and needed a buffer, someone to ward off problems from reaching him. That was Tannen's job. Unfortunately, she did more than handle conflicts: she created them. She would stand guard in front of the dressing room wherever they were appearing and with a stare virtually prohibit any of us who worked with them from ever entering to be socially friendly. She wanted total control over their very existence, and made sure to exercise that control in all situations. Her one saving grace, albeit miniscule, was that she was a dog lover. I think that was the only positive emotion she ever showed. It was as if the Lawrences were her own family, and she dedicated twenty-four hours a day to serving them. Unfortunately, her services created a host of antagonized people.

Those who aren't in the entertainment industry imagine that this sort of traveling and overall lifestyle is all fun and games. I'd like to set the record straight by saying it ain't so! As an example of some of the unseen downsides, whenever we would appear at one of the gambling casinos in Las Vegas or Atlantic City, our rooms would be complimentary and the house would issue us passes to the employees' dining room which was usually buried somewhere in the bowels of the building. We'd have to take an elevator to the basement, and then wander through a labyrinth of tunnels and passageways that would eventually culminate in a massive cafeteria, full of nearly inedible slop. Some were better than others, but the one in Caesars in Atlantic City was aptly dubbed *The Vomitorium,* in keeping with the Roman Empire scheme. The reason behind this scenario was that unless you happened to be a high roller, the prices in the restaurants were not suited for those of us who were there to earn a few dollars. A decent dinner would be anywhere from $50 to $70, and the breakfasts and lunches weren't all that much cheaper. We knew that unless food was provided, we'd barely be able to break even at the end of a week's work. The cafeterias were free so it made the engagement profitable financially but certainly not gastronomically pleasant.

Unfortunately, by the Millennium, the nightclubs that used to feature performers of the stature of Steve and Eydie had all vanished into the memories of those of us old enough to recall the '50s and the '60s. The Miami hotels had become condominiums for grousing seniors, the Theatres-in-the-Round became churches, the old Copacabana in New York had become a catering hall, the Latin Quarter was razed, and this left only the gambling towns as havens for the major stars. Since I'm not a gambler, it was unpleasant to have to spend my days sitting in a hotel room, wondering what the *vomitorium* had for the dinner special. Maybe it would be *Mule entrails fried in tar* or something equally as delicious.

In time, sadly, even the Las Vegas spots faded away. The town stopped being a haven for top entertainers and instead, developed into a "family fun place." The clientele stopped wearing chic garments, and the casinos were packed instead with busloads of senior citizens, farm workers and tours of semi-indigent people pouring quarters into the one-armed bandits. Las Vegas became an attraction not for the entertainment it could provide, but for the faux architecture of the theme-style hotels. One could visit the pyramids in Egypt by staying at the *Luxor,* a hotel shaped like a pyramid. Perhaps if the hoteliers had done some research they would have discovered that there were no pyramids in Luxor, only the Sphinx. (The pyramids were just outside Cairo.) One could see a replica of the Eiffel Tower at the Hotel *Paris.* One could visit Italy by journeying through the *Venetian.* One could also see impersonators of deceased entertainers; Elvis impressionists abounded; The "Rat Pack" was resuscitated with imitators of Sinatra, Lawford, Davis, Martin, etc., all dead. Very few of the old showroom entertainers were still featured in Las Vegas. Most had gone to the big stage in the sky. Wayne Newton was alive (to some extent, depending on one's viewpoint) and was a fixture at the Stardust. A tourist would go back home to Podunk and say he'd been all over the globe and seen all the biggest stars, while never having left the illusionary desert tract known as "Glitter Gulch."

In their final year, Steve & Eydie closed the showroom of Caesars Palace in Las Vegas, a room they had opened thirty-five years earlier. The powers-that-be at Caesars had concluded that they could fill the casino and hotel with or without star entertainment, so they decided to take the cavernous space that was the showroom and turn it into luxury suites for the high rollers. The ranting of Judy Tannen at a closing night party soured the management toward Steve & Eydie, and subsequently they were not offered spots at any of the other Vegas establishments owned by the parent company. At one point during the party while the invitees were reveling, someone got up to make a speech. Tannen grabbed the microphone and shouted, "Everyone shut the f—k up!" This was widely reported in a Las Vegas newspaper by a reporter who was there to cover the event. That was not an unusual occurrence. It would take an adding machine to count the number of locales that the duo was no longer welcome because of unnecessary scenes caused by Tannen's eruptions and demands. No one can convince me that over a forty-year span of their association with Tannen, Steve and Eydie were ignorant of her behavior, and I'll never understand exactly why they abided the whole scene.

The catastrophic events of September 11th, 2001 made the flying scene even more complex. With the advent of the extra security, it meant getting to an airport two to three hours in advance, depending on the size of the city. Waiting in endless lines to be searched, patted down and frisked was not something I anticipated with any joy. So when Steve made the announcement that he and Eydie were calling it the end of a career, at least for the time being, I was not saddened. A sense of relief came over me, and at the same time I felt a bit melancholy knowing that the type of music on which I had been weaned, the music that was gloriously orchestrated and sung, had come one step closer to vanishing.

In all honesty, I was relieved at the news that I'd no longer have to join the "Dynamic Duo" in far reaches of the country. I now could spend more time in the home environment that I love, and not have to be a party to the "unfriendly skies."

CHAPTER 19

THE OTHER SIDE OF THE LADDER

People with extended families that include children and grandchildren have a series of built-in yardsticks to let them know that they're getting older. When the grandchildren reach college age, the grandparents are forced to take a realistic look at each other, which will most often drive home the fact that they're turning into geezers and geezer-ettes. Not so with Shirley and me. Our decision not to have a family has allowed us to look into the mirror and see a few wrinkles and sags here and there, but it really doesn't tell us the whole true story. We delude ourselves into seeing what we remember of a more youthful era. The only way I can evaluate my true age is by the fact that I disapprove of just about everything that youngsters are doing. That goes for haircuts, body-piercing, car stereos spewing rap at jet-engine decibel levels, clothing styles, jargon and just about everything else that trendy youth seems to find fascinating.

For reasons unknown, I often think of my Grandpa Tebeau, who was unwittingly a surrogate father during my boyhood. He was the only male family figure who was always there, although perhaps not of his choosing. He was not a happy man and lived his life wishing he'd never encountered my grandmother. I'm sure that if women of that era could have been self-supporting (in the workplace,) he would have left for greener pastures. He had a dead-end job as a clerk in a brokerage office for thirty years and moonlighted every Sunday from 5 PM to midnight at the New York Times as a telegrapher. He worked the second job in order to make enough money for a one-week fishing vacation in Canada each year, which was the only time he could get far away from my grandmother. It was a miserable existence.

What brings him to mind is the fact that at my current age I have outlived him. The last few years of his life he was an old man.... a very old man. At the time he had hardening of the arteries, diagnosed today as a buildup of plaque due to excessive cholesterol. After his commute home on the subway, he'd ride the bus for only three long blocks. From that point he would walk the three short blocks from the bus stop to our house in Brooklyn and have to stop at least four times for a couple of minutes and lean against a tree to catch his breath. He'd make it inside the front door, put down the copy of the New York Daily News, sit in his easy chair and sleep until called to dinner. Not only did this alleviate his fatigue, it kept my grandmother from having the opportunity to nag him. At age sixty-seven, he succumbed to heart disease.

I look at myself having come through that time portal, but I don't see this aging body being anywhere near as beaten down and saddened as that old man I called "Dad." The mere awareness of better nutrition and exercise, plus decades of vitamin supplement therapy has kept me in a much more vital condition emotionally, mentally and physically. I worry because I inherited my grandfather's body, that non-muscular frame with no discernable waistline. If that portion of my genetic structure was a point of vulnerability, I felt sure I'd develop similar symptoms of degeneration. Luckily, that hasn't been the case.

If he'd been a bit more sophisticated and worldly, Grandpa Tebeau would have been a first-rate curmudgeon. I liken him both physically and disposition-wise to the late W. C. Fields. He could find a negative factor in anyone or anything, and make a clever case against whatever or whoever may have been his target. I'm afraid some this trait carried over to me, although I try to make it more acceptable by using humor in conjunction with my comments. I've expanded on that characteristic by becoming a prolific writer of letters-to-the-editor. My periodic opinionated ranting gets published in the *Island Packet*, Hilton Head's daily newspaper. Gramps was never big on kids or pets or anything that might interrupt his naps. I must admit to having inherited that set of values as well, never wanting to own anything that has to be fed, watered, walked or medicated.

I find myself at a stage of life when I'm attempting to tie together various elements that were instrumental to my development. I'm hoping to create a genealogical blueprint along with an album of old family photos and tintypes dating back to the nineteenth century. Perhaps it's a way for me to reconnect to my heritage and to put my life's influences into some perspective. I personally enjoy photo albums from the past. I have always made a point of keeping scrapbooks and photo albums from my first band at age fourteen up until the present. In one sense they're enjoyable to peruse, but in another, they define the time line that I really don't care to see. The early photos magnify the teen-age pimples. As for the most recent photos, I bemoan the fact that the lighting wasn't better, and how they show up the eye bags, jowls and double chin. There are a myriad of pictures inserted into the clear plastic sleeves of the albums, some starting to turn a light amber from age along with the acid content in the photo papers. The hairstyles combined with the length of sideburns act as an undated calendar.

Some personalities have been classified by psychiatrists and therapists by being given letters to identify characteristics. If I were to guess my own, it's now a "type L", for lazy. I'm certainly not a "type A", as I do not have a competitive drive, nor did I ever enjoy playing or watching contact sports. As a student in grammar school, my teachers constantly chided me as one who's IQ level was far above my scholastic achievements and because I was lazy. My marks were poor. Maybe the teachers were right. Someone once facetiously asked if I ever studied indifference, to which I replied,

"No, but I majored in lethargy."

I had an ulterior motive for choosing the world of music as my vocation. The piano came easily, and I didn't have to work hard or study to achieve my goals, nor did I have to knock on doors to pursue employment. Employment usually found me. As any newcomer to the music business will invariably find out, jobs are few and far between. They also don't pay especially well for those who are as yet unproven, so we tend to develop the automatic "yes" syndrome. As a neophyte, whenever a job was offered, I answered in the affirmative for fear I may not work again the remainder of the year. The unfortunate side to this behavior is that I didn't realize it until fifty years later when I found myself still doing the very same thing. Here I am, after almost fifty-five years of success still saying yes to just about everything that is offered. The afterthoughts are usually regrets that I automatically accepted the offer and the realization that I have yet to learn how to say a polite, "No thanks."

One of life's greatest joys is waking up leisurely in the morning, knowing I have a clear schedule for the day. That hasn't happened too often, and I can mainly attribute it to the law of supply and demand. I have certain talents that are in short supply for the music lovers who reside in my area, and rather than disappoint the people whose taste keeps good music by good composers alive, I will generally accept the chance to play for them. To say "no" may be some sort of selfish advantage, but it can often make for an unhappy group of admirers. Knowing this, I may never really acquire the knack of refusing. Only time will tell.

I know one thing for certain: I definitely intend to cut back on my volume of engagements, and will try to focus on the ones that provide the least pressure. Yes, pressure. One may not always be aware of it, but every job adds a layer of anxiety to my psyche. If I'm acting as a leader, pressure is finding talented, reliable personnel who will show up on time, properly attired. My idea of being "on time" is to arrive at least thirty minutes before the job begins. Musicians who arrive three minutes before the downbeat have always driven me up the wall! As much as I enjoy playing, the business end leaves me cold. The whole time I was in Hollywood, I had a contractor for every show on which I was the leader. His job was to call the personnel with the times and uniforms (if any dress code applied), compute all the salaries, do the bookkeeping and make out the paychecks for the musicians, leaving me free to deal only with the music, not the business. Having a contractor was dictated by the musicians union, who also insisted that a cartage company deliver and pick up any heavy instruments to and from the various venues. Since the Hilton Head area has a less-than-strong union presence, those types of clauses are nowhere to be found. One of my pet peeves is hauling around an electric piano, amplifier, seat, keyboard stand and accessory kit. That may be an accepted part of the music business for the under-forty set who grew up with guitars, amps, sound systems and drum kits, but for one who spent his life walking in to a well-tuned grand piano on-site, it doesn't sit too well. Probably one of the first things I will change when I begin to downsize my schedule is the carting of a keyboard. If there's a piano at the venue, I'll gladly play it. If not, then someone had better get a hefty, muscular individual to carry this load and bring it back after the job's finished! Weight lifting has never been one of my assets. When I was young, I was once referred to by one of my peers as "One hundred and eighty pounds of fat and bone. Not an ounce of muscle to be seen." As I reach the later stages of life, that description has remained constant. Only the location of the fat has shifted due to gravity.

Another anxiety creator is the acceptance of an engagement where I have been highly touted and publicized, which in my mind means I have to be exceedingly successful in pulling it off. I refer to theatrical and stage presentations. As great as they seem to the audiences, the months of planning that precede the actual performances are quite stressful. The amount of rehearsal time generally allocated is far less than adequate, and I usually find myself flying by the seat of my pants. I will no longer accept positions of musical director where employment with name performers is concerned, but rather that of just plain pianist. The musical director has to be responsible for the artist's music library, attend all the meetings before and after every performance, and take the brunt of the artist's adrenaline variances. To a performer, tempos are almost always too fast or too slow. Even proving the tempos were consistent with a metronome will never convince the person onstage that you did it exactly as it was rehearsed. The musical director has to swallow his pride and acquiesce. That may have been something that I could cope with many years ago, but I refuse to spend my golden years having to deal with artist's egos. I prefer to simply walk onstage, play the piano part as best I can, and when the show is over, go my merry way.

When I mention to friends that I enjoy doing "nothing," they can't understand it. The truth is that a day of "nothing" is usually filled, but with non-scheduled events. I can find pleasure just washing the car, or browsing a supermarket while trying to come up with what to make for dinner. The late afternoon snooze is a great pleasure, along with the five-o-clock glass of a good single-malt scotch. It really doesn't take a lot to make me appreciate how good life can be. This may be a manifestation of the lazy part of me, but whatever it may be, I can comfortably accept and enjoy it.

Doing "nothing" also allows me to be the curmudgeon who is always writing letters to the editor chiding the politicians and nabobs on some of their less-than-thoughtful decisions. I take great pleasure in getting off a blast now and again. I may be considered by some to be a "crabapple," although I feel compelled to hide that side of my personality to the world in general. I have an extended list of basic annoyances ranging from people who allow their cell phones to chirp while dining in a restaurant or jazz club, then proceed to answer them and carry on a conversation, to those who use the phones while trying to one-hand the steering wheel of an oversized behemoth of an SUV. I own a cell phone, and most months the bill shows no usage. It's kept for emergencies only, since I do a lot of back-road commuting at night. I'm also from an era when slovenliness was frowned upon, and despite the fashion magazines telling me a four-day stubble is today's look, I still don't buy it. Clothes may be casual, but should be clean and color coordinated. Am I sounding like an old fuddy-duddy?

Perhaps it's because in reality, I am. Maybe I simply believe in good manners such as removing those nerdy-looking backward-billed baseball caps when sitting down to dine in a restaurant. I prefer a chilled pilsner glass from which to quaff my brew, as I still can't get myself to swill it down from a longneck bottle. Nor do I appreciate the art of tattooing on the bodies of otherwise attractive young men and women. It is said that a person knows he's getting old when the trendiness of the day is unacceptable. I howl about the mode of dress, the rap-spewing boom-box speakers in cars and the general decline in civility, but I guess it's really not that different than my younger years. As a youth I'd listen to 45 r.p.m. records of Stan Kenton's orchestra playing Bob Graettinger's "City of Glass," a rather dissonant series of what were purported to be futuristic compositions. This would invariably elicit bellows from my grandparents who had been reared on the music of John Philip Sousa and Rudolph Friml. Music is definitely the greatest generational separator, and has become a weapon, a wedge that adolescents wield against the mores and tastes of their parents.

It's approaching my time to sit back, relax and smell the roses. If I plan carefully, the ensuing years should allow for me to do just that more frequently. I'll never leave the world of music totally. I don't think a musician actually can, nor would I truly choose to. I feel as if I was born into music, and it's with me throughout every waking moment. Sometimes it's playing on the stereo, other times it's in my head. I made a point of telling Shirley early in our relationship that I had a mistress. This mistress would be around forever. Her name is *Music.*

I feel very fortunate to live on Hilton Head and to have the opportunity to play with some of the finest musicians in the area, among them legendary bassist Ben Tucker, guitarist Bruce Spradley and percussionist Steve Primatic to name only a few. If all goes well there'll be some pleasant jazz performances with fine players in the future, and one hopes some intriguing vacations with Shirley. Stay tuned for more to come!

Does it feel as if I was born fifty years too late? Maybe I

was. In the meantime, I guess I'll just go down to the corner, grab a horse-car and go home. If I'm lucky, I'll remember to pick up the Ginko Biloba on the way!

"Twenty-three skidoo!"